After college, Montgomery Worshack—Monty—ran away from the life his parents had planned for him and became an elite circus performer. Working hard, he becomes a headliner, and he loves every second of it. When his trapeze breaks while he's training for a new trick, his life is turned upside down. While he's lying in the hospital with a fractured leg, his parents descend, trying to take over.

Fortunately, Monty's friends arrive, too. With one being a doctor—Morgan Pruitt—they whisk him away from his interfering parents and take him home with them. Monty knows he has months of healing and therapy ahead of him before he can even think about training to find a new circus position. To alleviate the boredom, he accepts Morgan's invitation to join him at the wedding of his friend's son—Jake Lewis. While there, Monty finds his attention snagged by a very handsome police officer, Brian O'Reilly.

Considering how hot Brian finds Monty, he can't help relaxing the injured man in the best possible of ways. After that, he doesn't return the man's call. Brian has been burned before. He has no desire to get involved with another man who's sure to leave him for greener pastures. Except, when Brian learns that Monty's father is making threats, he can't stay away.

Can Brian guard his heart while helping secure Monty's safety?

This book is a work of fiction. Names, characters, places, and incidents either are products of the author's imagination or are used fictitiously. Any resemblance to actual events or locales or persons, living or dead, is entirely coincidental.

Two-Handed Clutch
Copyright © 2023 Charlie Richards
ISBN: 978-1-4874-3839-5
Cover art by Angela Waters

Published by eXtasy Books Inc

Look for us online at:
www.eXtasybooks.com

Two-Handed Clutch
Carry Me: Book Thirteen

By

Charlie Richards

DEDICATION

*Slow and steady may not win the race, but it will get you to the
finish line.*
~Me

CHAPTER ONE

Monty Worshack couldn't decide what woke him first — the incessant *beep, beep, beep* of the machines or the pain radiating through his body.

What the hell happened?

Even as the thought entered his agony-riddled mind, Monty recalled . . . everything. Fear spiked within him as he remembered the sound of the trapeze line snapping. The feel of air rushing past his face had taken his breath away, and not in the way he relished. Monty had screamed as he'd seen the floor of the practice tent rushing toward him, his mind blanking in disbelief as he spotted the fallen left corner of the safety net.

Snapping his eyelids open, Monty panted softly as he stared at the ceiling. As expected, it was a sterile white. Still, that view was better than the memory reel playing across the backs of his eyelids.

Monty slowed his breathing, doing his best to push those thoughts from his mind. Instead, he counted the paint globs within his field of vision. He also focused on each measured exhalation, imagining with each breath out that he was expelling the pain, allowing him to beat back the waves of agony buffeting his body.

"Well, hello, Mister Worshack," a feminine voice greeted, heralding the arrival of a nurse. A blonde's smiling face appeared in Monty's line of sight. "We're so very pleased to see you awake."

We? What we?

1

Monty only saw *her*.

As the woman shown a light into Monty's eyes, she told him, "My name's Nurse Matilda, and I imagine you have a few questions." She put the light away before patting his wrist. "I'll let Doctor Lorrenz know you're awake. I'm certain your family will be pleased to hear it, too."

Family?

Wait. What?

Wanting to question her, Monty opened his mouth. His voice came out a quiet rasp as he muttered, "Wait." Fortunately, that was enough to catch the nurse's attention, and she turned back to face him. "W-Water," Monty forced out.

"Just a little," Nurse Matilda told him, crossing to a side table. "We don't want your stomach upset."

Whatever.

Monty opened his mouth when she offered him the straw. He sucked down two mouthfuls before he noticed her pulling it away. Managing another half a mouthful before she could get the straw out of his mouth, Monty rolled that across his tongue for a few seconds.

When Nurse Matilda patted his shoulder lightly and told him, "Be back in a minute," Monty swallowed the water.

"What family?" Monty managed to ask.

Nurse Matilda paused and smiled at him once more. "Your parents, of course."

Oh fuck.

Monty's brain stalled at that news. Nothing good ever came from him dealing with his parents. Monty hadn't seen them in over a decade. Instead, he used a lawyer to converse with them.

Before Monty could order them away from him, Nurse Matilda was gone.

Shit.

Blowing out a breath, Monty returned his focus to the ceiling. His mind began to drift, and he realized he had to be on pretty heavy pain meds. Blinking quickly, Monty did his best to focus. If his parents were allowed in the room, he knew he would need his wits about him, pain or not.

Monty slowly turned his head, looking left and right. It took two sweeps over the sides of his bed to spot the call button. He moved his right hand, and a fresh wave of pain stabbed through him.

That was when Monty registered the cast on his right wrist. Growling softly, he glared at the offending item that covered his arm from below his elbow to his palm. Monty bit back a growl of frustration as he wondered why the hell the remote with the call button would be set up on the same side of his bed as his injured wrist.

Breathing deeply, Monty lifted his arm. He felt sweat break out on his temples and brow as he reached for the device. As he pressed the button with his forefinger, causing a spike of agony to erupt up his arm, the heartrate monitor beside his bed went off, filling the air with more and more beeps.

Damn annoying machine.

Hearing the sound of running footsteps, whether in response to the call button or the incessant beeps, Monty didn't know and didn't care. All he cared about was the fact that a man in hospital scrubs came rushing into the room. Nurse Matilda was right behind him.

"Easy now, Mister Worshack," the guy soothed, stopping beside the bed. He glanced at the machine, then stared down at Monty. "Take a few nice deep breaths for me. I can't give you more pain meds quite yet. It'll be another hour, so let's try to relax a little on your own." His dark eyes held a note of concern. "Seeing as you just woke up, I really don't want to have to sedate you."

Monty did as the man ordered, easily getting his pulse back under control. Hell, controlling his pulse—and nerves—had become a way of life for him. Ever since Monty had taken up gymnastics when he was seven years old, he'd learned to regulate his breathing.

"That's good, Mister Worshack," the man encouraged. "Very good." He smiled at Monty. "Oh, I'm Doctor Lorrenz, by the way." The doctor chuckled, a wry smile curving his lips. "Now, let's go over what happened. Shall we?" Before Monty could hope to answer, Doctor Lorrenz added, "I've already gone over your care and next steps with your parents, and they've assured me you'll have plenty of help, so try not to panic upon hearing anything I tell you, okay, Mister Worshack?"

Scowling at Doctor Lorrenz, Monty finally found his tongue. "My parents are not my emergency contact. Why did you call them?"

"I don't recall who called them or why," Doctor Lorrenz stated slowly. He rested one hand on Monty's shoulder and lifted the other in placation. "That was done while I was in surgery with you."

Monty didn't care for that response—not in the least. "We're estranged," he admitted with a grimace. "Please don't tell them anything more about my condition, and don't allow them in my room."

While Doctor Lorrenz appeared surprised, he nodded once. "Of course, Mister Worshack." The doctor looked at the nurse. "Put that in his file, and contact security, just in case."

A wide-eyed Nurse Matilda nodded swiftly before scribbling something on the chart she'd been holding. Then she stuck her head out of the room and called to someone.

"And call me Monty." With a curl of his lip, Monty grumbled, "Mister Worshack is my father."

"As you wish, Mister, uh, Monty." Doctor Lorrenz quickly amended his words. Then he smiled at Monty again, his expression one of encouragement. "Let's go over your injuries."

For the next few minutes, Monty listened as Doctor Lorrenz detailed what had happened to him. In all his years of gymnastics and circus performing, he'd never broken anything. Many had commented on how lucky he was.

Guess my luck finally ran out.

Monty learned he had micro-tears in the tendons of his right wrist, hence the cast. The recovery time on that was only a few weeks before he would be able to use it lightly again. The doctor stressed *light duty only.*

Unfortunately, Monty's left leg was another thing altogether. The break in his tibia had been clean and easily set. His fibula, however, had several fractures in it, and the doctor had used a metal plate and screws to reconstruct it. Monty would have months of healing as well as therapy ahead of him.

God, that sucks.

At least I'm alive.

Monty knew that it could have been so much worse. He didn't know how the corner of the safety net had come loose, leaving the area he'd landed at only a foot above the floor. With his momentum, if he'd landed headfirst, he could easily have died.

Instead, it'll just take a little time for me to walk again, but I will.

Besides, I don't need my legs to practice on a swing in a month or so after my wrist heals.

"I know it can seem overwhelming, Monty." The doctor patted his shoulder, perhaps to soothe or to get his attention. "But try to remember that you were very fortunate."

Monty snapped his focus back to the doctor and managed to give the man a small smile. "I know I was fortunate," he told him quietly. "I'll heal."

Doctor Lorrenz returned his smile as he nodded once more. Then his expression faded to be replaced with a worried furrowing to his brows. "You'll need assistance, however. If not your parents, do you have—"

"What do you mean I can't see my son?" A high-pitched, angry feminine voice carried into the room. It was a voice Monty recognized all too well—his mother, Veronica Worshack. "I was told he'd woken. I demand you step aside and—"

"I'm sorry, ma'am," a deep voice countered. "But if a patient requests someone be barred from the room, then we are duty-bound to enforce his wishes. Son or not, you and your husband cannot enter."

"What the bloody hell are you talking about?" another man all but bellowed. "Montgomery is our son. You can't bar us from our son. He's drug-addled and doesn't know what he's talking about."

And that's my father — Cornelian Worshack — a man who thinks his word is law.

"I'm very sorry, sir," the other male stated again, his voice deep and firm. "Until we hear otherwise from the patient, I can't let you in there."

"You will get out of my way," Cornelian demanded again. "Or this hospital will be hearing from my lawyer."

Yup. That's normal, too.

"God, he's such an ass," Monty mumbled. When he saw Doctor Lorrenz's brows rise high on his forehead while Nurse Matilda lifted a hand to cover her mouth as she snickered, he realized he'd said that out loud. *Okay. So maybe I am a little drug-addled. It's still true.* With a shrug, Monty murmured, "Sorry. It's true. If he doesn't get his way, he threatens."

"Well, lawyer or not, our policy is clear," Doctor Lorrenz stated with a frown. After hearing a still-threatening Cornelian and an indignant-sounding Veronica move away, their voices getting softer until they were gone, Doctor Lorrenz cleared his throat and told Monty, "That still brings us back to you needing assistance for a while. Do you—"

"Monty!" another feminine voice cried, heralding the arrival of several people barreling into his room. "What the hell happened?"

Relief filled Monty as three women rushed to his bedside. A blond man soon joined them while a second hung back. The dark-haired, bearded man swept his gaze around the area, taking in everything as if checking the room for danger.

"Hi, guys," Monty murmured, smiling as relief flooded him. He glanced between the trio of women — Donna, Naomi, and Jenna — friends he'd known since before college. Then Monty looked at the blond male — Morgan — who he'd met through the trio during his second year. "I'm so damn glad to see you all."

"The second they called me, I rounded up the gang," Donna declared. She was his emergency contact, had been since he'd graduated college and run away to join the circus.

"Thank you all for coming." Monty sighed deeply, finally able to begin to relax now that he had his friends there. "I appreciate you dropping everything and flying halfway across the country for me."

His friends still resided in southwestern Oregon in the medium-sized town they'd grown up in. While Monty still owned a house there — passed onto him by his grandfather, much to his parents' fury — he didn't visit often. His life on the road with the circus didn't leave much room to schedule visits. Currently, the circus was a little north of Birmingham, Alabama.

Naomi blew a very unladylike raspberry. The redhead had always had a fiery personality. "Of course, we'd come." She rested her hands on the side of the bed and leaned close to him. "If you weren't laid up, I'd smack you upside the head."

Monty winced. "Thanks for not doing that." As much as he appreciated her feistiness, he'd been the recipient of her smacks before. They hurt.

"How long before he can travel, doctor?" Morgan asked. He rested his hand on the calf of Monty's good leg and squeezed. "Ryan rented a large van, and we'll drive you home."

"And we need to be back to town by the eighth, or Carl will have my head," the dark-haired bearded man stated, a smirk curving his lips. "I'm Ryan Straton, by the way." He used a thumb to point toward Morgan. "This one's partner."

Monty had figured that. A few years before, Morgan had run into a little trouble. The detective had helped him out, and they'd struck up a hot fling that had turned into more. Now they were a committed couple, and when Morgan smiled at Ryan, Monty could see the love shining in both their eyes as they stared at each other.

"Sorry, hero," Morgan stated. "I should have introduced you."

"It's fine, babe." Ryan slipped his arm around Morgan's waist proprietarily. "You have other things on your mind."

Morgan winced as he returned his attention to Monty. "And we definitely want to know what the hell happened to you."

Both Morgan and Donna were doctors, and Monty saw the way both of them were running their gazes over him as if they had X-ray vision and could deduce his injuries just by looking.

With a sigh, Monty smiled vacantly. "Just my time to get hurt, I guess." When he saw Jenna rest her dark hands on her jeans-clad hips, he quickly added, "And I just woke up. I haven't even had time to talk to my boss, yet."

Arland Washburn was the ringmaster of the circus and a tough but fair man. Morgan needed to find out if he would have a place with them after he healed.

"We've put in a call to Mister Washburn, letting him know that you've woken," Nurse Matilda cut in. "He said to let you know that he would drop by this evening."

If Monty even knew what time it was — or what day — perhaps that would mean something to him.

"Uh, okay." Monty found his curiosity eating at him, and he focused on Ryan. "What's happening on the eighth?"

"My best friend's son is getting married," Ryan told him. With a chuckle, he added, "If I miss Jake's wedding, Carl will kill me." His dark eyes twinkled as he added, "And considering he's a fellow detective, he'll know how to dispose of my body so no one will ever find it."

Monty chuckled softly, but he stopped quickly. Even that hurt. He felt his head begin to swim as fatigue began to pull him under.

When he murmured, "You can tell these guys everything about my condition, doc," he could hear the slight slurring in his words.

Oh, well.

"You just rest, Monty," Donna encouraged, running her fingers through his short blond hair. "We'll take care of everything."

"Okay."

After that, Monty couldn't remember anything.

CHAPTER TWO

While catching the basketball, Brian O'Reilly used his peripheral vision to check the location of the nearest opponent. He spotted Vincent ten feet to his right and closing fast. Another firefighter, Trace, was to Brian's left. The bulky man had just pivoted and was starting toward him.

Brian turned and dribbled the ball up the court, searching for someone to pass it to even as he tried to get closer to the hoop. In another twenty feet, he could make a decent shot. Vincent caught up to him before that happened.

Fortunately, Brian spotted Lance up the court to his right. He palmed the ball and took a step to the left to dodge Vincent's grab at it. Then he snapped a quick pass to his fellow player.

Lance caught the ball, pivoted, and put it in the air.

Brian watched with a grin as the ball swished through the hoop.

"Nothin' but net, baby!" Lance crowed, hopping and grinning like a teenager. He bounded over to Brian and held up a hand.

Giving Lance a high-five, Brian grinned, too. "Nice shot, man."

"Thanks!" Lance smacked Brian on the ass as he stated, "Great throw."

Then Lance rushed toward where Vincent was getting ready to throw the ball back inbounds from near the net. Brian quickly followed, looking for his own opponent to block. He did his best to ignore the sting to his left butt cheek.

Brian knew that Lance didn't mean anything by it. His fellow police officer wasn't gay . . . or even bisexual. Instead, it was just camaraderie.

That meant Brian had to ignore the sudden perking of his dick. Not only would getting a boner be wholly inappropriate from Lance's unintentional teasing, it would be damn embarrassing. After all, considering Brian favored boxers, there was no way his sudden wood wouldn't be noticeable.

Yeah. No way I want to deal with the razzing that would cause.

Besides, Brian knew it was just because it'd been way too long since he'd gotten laid. He'd had a few one-night stands since Zack had left him, but most of the time, it was just too much effort. His hand worked just fine and didn't leave him feeling empty like he did after fucking some nameless, faceless stranger.

Fortunately, thoughts of his ex quickly caused his prick to deflate.

Good.

Brian hated that, even after over a year, thoughts of Zack still caused a reaction within him. Of course, these days, that reaction was to make his dick shrivel. Prior to his cheating ex's leaving, thoughts of Zack would have had the opposite effect.

Shoving thoughts of the asshole from his mind, Brian returned his attention to where it should be — their precinct basketball game against a team of firefighters.

It was just in time, too.

Vincent must have noticed Brian's inattention, for he'd just zinged the ball at Trace, who Brian was supposed to be guarding. He raced to the left, where Vincent had thrown the ball, obviously leading Trace away from him. With a lunge, Brian stretched out his arm. He barely managed to get his fingers on the ball, but it was enough. With a flick of his wrist, Brian shoved the ball to the right . . . right into Carl's advancing frame.

While Carl looked surprised, the detective recovered swiftly enough. He began to dribble while rushing down the court, back toward their opponent's hoop.

Brian didn't see the rest. He was too busy landing on his side, only to roll several feet. Once he rose, Brian looked down the court and grinned, seeing his teammates' high fives and hearing the others' congratulating Carl.

Sweet!

A glance at the scoreboard showed Brian that they were up by seven points.

Still, a small gap.

Brian hurried to join the others and get back in the game.

Flopping back on the bench at the side of the court, Brian tipped a water bottle to his mouth and squirted. The cold liquid poured into his mouth, soaking his dry tongue. A dribble overflowed, passing his lips and dripping down the heated flesh of his neck and chest.

Brian released the pressure, stopping the flow. Closing his mouth, he swished the liquid around his mouth before swallowing it. Then he quickly took another drink.

As Brian swallowed that, he returned his attention to the game before him. There were only a couple of minutes left in the fourth quarter, and the boys in blue were up over the firefighters. Brian hollered encouragement, but he knew he wouldn't have enough energy to get out there again.

Hell, his legs were trembling even as he sat on the bench.

Brian knew he should have come out a few minutes prior, but he'd been having so much fun . . . and he was hella competitive. He wanted to do everything in his power to help his fellow police officers beat the firefighter team. After all, they'd lost the last time, so he really wanted to stick it to 'em this time around.

Grinning, Brian watched Lance sink another basket. His

fellow cop was damn good. His score put his team up by fifteen points with only a minute to play.

We got this one.

Brian still managed to get to his feet, ignoring the fatigue and the slight twitching in his right leg's calf muscle. Hollering encouragement, grinning like a loon, he watched Macon—one of their crime scene photographers—sink another basket. A few seconds later, Chad—a guy who was surprisingly lean, toned, and agile for a computer specialist—stole the ball from another firefighter and passed it to Lance. Lance dribbled a few yards before passing it to Carl, who easily made the shot.

A few seconds later, the buzzer sounded, and they'd won the game.

Whooping and hollering, Brian welcomed the surge of adrenaline as he bounced onto the court. He patted his fellow officers on the back and pulled a couple into quick bro-hugs. Brian lined up with the rest and went through the process of giving gentle hand-slaps to the firefighters and murmuring, "Good game" to them all.

After that bit of good sportsmanship had been completed, Brian felt an arm wrap around his shoulders. He peered up the inch height difference and grinned at Vincent.

"Damn," Vincent rumbled. "You totally had me fooled earlier." With a wide smile and a shake of his head, he told him, "I really thought I'd caught you wool-gathering that one time, but you stole it and sent it to Carl."

Vincent laughed, obviously not upset, showing what a great sport the firefighter was.

Brian chuckled, shaking his head. "Actually, you *did* catch me wool-gathering," he admitted. "I just happened to snap out of it at the perfect time."

"I'll say." Trace appeared at Brian's other side. "Well played."

"Thanks." Brian barely resisted preening. After all, that

was not a good look on a thirty-four-year-old. "I got lucky on that one."

"Well, luck or not, it was a great game," Carl stated, joining them. He grabbed Vincent's waist and tugged him away from Brian—as if Brian would ever think of trying to steal the man's partner. "Good job, man. You've helped make my night look brighter than ever."

Confused, Brian cocked his head. "What's that supposed to mean?"

Trace groaned even as he grinned and shook his head. "Some things are better left not asked, Bri." Then he patted him on the back and began heading toward the bleachers. "See you later."

Following where Trace focused, Brian spotted the blond man standing at the base of the bleachers. He was handsome with sparkling green eyes that promised mischief . . . and fun. The heated look he was giving Trace was a clear indicator of what he wanted to do to the man.

Brian yanked his attention away from the pair as Trace wrapped his arms around his partner—Laramie. He did his best to squash the jealousy that began churning in his gut. He wasn't jealous of Laramie or Trace, per se. Instead, he just really wanted what they had.

Hell, what Carl and Vincent have, too.

Thought I had it with Zack, but—

Once more, Brian ruthlessly stamped down thoughts of his ex.

God, it's been over a year. Get over yourself.

After a quick, chaste kiss, Carl peeled away from Vincent and headed toward the locker room utilized by the police officers.

"Hey, what happened to Ryan tonight?" Brian asked, following Carl along the row of lockers. "First time he's missed a game."

Carl winced and nodded. "He and his man were called out

of town a few days ago. Emergency." Lifting a switch, he opened his locker as he kept talking. "One of Morgan's best friends ended up in the hospital."

Brian nodded slowly, opening his locker and pulling out a large bottle of water and a towel. "Is Morgan's friend okay?"

He knew that Morgan was Ryan's partner. The man was also an exceptional doctor. Morgan had patched up Brian on more than one occasion when the shit had hit the fan.

Grimacing, Carl shook his head. "In time," he stated non-committedly. "Monty ended up with a fractured leg. Surgery, metal plates, screws, the works."

Brian winced in sympathy as he poured water onto his towel after he'd stripped off his shirt. As he began giving himself a swift wipe-down, he asked, "Damn. What happened?"

"Trapeze line broke," Carl told him. "And the safety net wasn't secured properly. Monty's lucky he didn't land on his head."

"Trapeze line," Brian repeated, freezing. "Huh?"

Carl focused on Brian, his hazel eyes widening a little. "Oh. Monty's a trapeze artist in a traveling circle. A headliner, from what I heard." With a soft laugh, Carl smiled. "Guess he ran away to the circus right after college. Who does that anymore?"

"Huh." Brian didn't have a response to that.

Who indeed?

"Well, I hope Monty ends up okay," Brian went with.

Nodding, Carl silently agreed. Then he patted the back of his hand against Brian's upper arm. "You coming on Saturday to Jake's wedding?"

Brian instantly nodded. "Yeah. Wouldn't miss it."

Jake was Carl's son. The guy had been living with his partner, Devon, for nearly five years. When introduced, they referred to each other as husband. This was just a formality to get the piece of paper, but Brian had heard that Jake and Devon were looking forward to it.

15

As much as watching another gay couple get married would stir up his own jealousy, Brian wouldn't have missed it for the world.

"Good. Jake appreciates the support," Carl told him.

Smiling, Brian rubbed a dry section of the towel over himself. "You raised a good one." Then he sobered and asked, "Is your ex-wife going to be there?"

While it had been before Brian's time on the force, he'd heard that Rhonda, Carl's ex, had done her best to seduce plenty of officers while trying to undermine Carl. She'd been a vindictive bitch when Carl had started dating Vincent. Fortunately, with the help of a good child-custody lawyer, helping beat any possible prejudices, Carl had retained partial custody of his kids.

"Hell, no," Carl grumbled. "Rhonda cut Jake out of her life when he moved in with Devon." A muscle ticked in his jaw, but he didn't say more.

Brian wouldn't have had that much restraint if he were talking about his ex.

Cheating bastard.

Pushing thoughts of Zack aside once more—*I must really need to get laid to be thinking about him so much*—Brian asked, "Is Ryan going to make it back in time for the wedding?"

Brian knew that Ryan was like an uncle to Jake. He was part of Carl's family.

Fortunately, that was something Brian still had. When he'd come out, his parents and siblings hadn't turned their back on him.

"Yeah. Ryan and Morgan are already on their way back. Driving from Alabama with Morgan's friends," Carl told him as he lifted a shirt over his head. "They'll be here."

Nodding, Brian started pulling on his own clean clothes. "I know Jake will appreciate that."

Carl was busy tugging on a pair of jeans, so he just grunted in acknowledgment.

Brian stared around the large backyard, taking in the decorations of navy blues and greens. Balloons were everywhere. Even the trees ringing the impressive space held stringers of ribbons in the same colors.

Good god. Did a party store vomit blue and green decorations?

Just as the thought popped into his head, Brian mentally grimaced.

Ugh. I should not be thinking such thoughts at a wedding. This is supposed to be a joyous occasion.

Fortunately, the sound of the wedding march caught Brian's attention. He rose to his feet and peered toward the back deck. Brian immediately spotted Jake standing there. Between the joy on his grinning face and the fine cut of his white suit, he looked damn handsome.

Carl stood beside him, sporting a proud expression. The pair headed down the couple of steps off the back deck and made their way up the aisle between the rows of chairs. Their destination was the arbor which had been set up at the other end.

And Devon.

The broad-shouldered, dark-skinned man's attention was riveted on his approaching husband-to-be.

Well, I guess technically, Jake is already Devon's husband.

While chatting with others before the wedding, Brian had learned that, a couple of years before, Devon had proposed to Jake, who'd accepted. While Jake hadn't wanted planning a wedding, then a honeymoon, to take his focus away from his college studies, the young man hadn't wanted to wait, either. Jake and Devon had gone before the Justice of the Peace and tied the knot.

Finally, after finishing his degree, Jake was getting the wedding of his dreams.

Once the pair reached the front and Carl handed off Jake to Devon, everyone sat and the ceremony began.

Brian relaxed in his chair and listened as his attention drifted over the gathered crowd. Devon came from a large family—four brothers and a single father, and they were all in attendance, most of them with dates. Jake had a slew of friends, and his younger sister, Lorna, was the maid of honor. Just like Brian, a number of Carl and Vincent's friends were there to support Jake, who'd watched him grow into a fine man over the years after Carl had divorced his wife, Rhonda.

Rhonda, as expected, was absent. Carl's ex was a bigot, not approving of homosexuality, and was quite vocal about it, from what Brian had heard. Brian had overheard Carl telling Ryan that Jake hadn't even invited her.

Probably a good call.

Brian found his attention snagged by a blond man to his left. He was a couple of rows up in a wheelchair, which had been parked at the end. A short cast covered his right arm, and Brian noticed a much larger cast encasing his left leg peeking out from the blanket covering his lap. Considering Morgan sat in the chair beside him, Brian guessed the stranger to be Monty, the man who'd been picked up in Alabama.

As Brian heard the man officiating the wedding announce the couple as husband and husband, he had a hard time pulling his gaze away from the injured blond's handsome profile.

Damn. He's pretty.

Then everyone rose once more to watch Jake and Devon Gateman head back down the aisle, blocking Brian's view.

Brian focused on the pair and clapped along with the others, doing his best to keep a relaxed smile pasted on his lips.

CHAPTER THREE

M onty listened to Jake and Devon exchange vows. When
Morgan had invited him to the wedding, he'd only
agreed so he could get out of the house for a while. He'd been
home a couple of days and was already going stir-crazy due
to the forced inactivity.

Taking in the love clearly filling Jake and Devon's expressions as they looked at each other, Monty pondered what it
would be like to be on the receiving end of such intense feelings. He'd never been in a relationship before. Monty had enjoyed plenty of sex over the years and had even benefited
from a fuck-buddy arrangement with a fellow circus performer, but there'd never existed any feelings between himself and any one of them.

He knew he wasn't getting any younger, and after healing,
he knew getting a new position with a circus would be tough.
There weren't that many around anymore, and competition
was fierce—and most of them were younger.

Monty couldn't blame Ringmaster Arland for telling him
that he couldn't hold his position for him. In truth, Monty appreciated the straight answer. He knew where he stood, and
he could plan his future accordingly.

In fact, Monty had already started searching for ads. He
knew any positions he spotted now wouldn't be available by
the time he finished with his rehab. Instead, Monty wanted to
keep an eye on the job market to see what sort of opportunities he could expect.

Monty had even spotted an opening for a dancer who

knew aerial silks located in Las Vegas. It had occurred to him that his skills as a trapeze artist might traverse over to that. He wasn't too keen on the idea of living in the desert heat, though.

Morgan, rising to his feet to his right, pulled Monty out of his thoughts. Focusing on the happy couple, he managed to glimpse them between the standing people. They moved down the aisle, arms around each other's waists, grinning broadly.

Definitely happy.

Smiling faintly, Monty couldn't imagine the kinds of feelings that would be needed to not only devote himself to one person, but for him to trust that person enough to return his devotion. His own parents certainly weren't good role models for a healthy, loving relationship. The pair acted more like business partners. In fact, if nothing had changed from Monty's teenage years, his parents didn't even share the same bedroom.

Not that I've been home since going away to college to confirm that's still the case.

And I sure as hell don't want to.

"Are you ready for food, Monty?" Morgan asked, turning to him with a smile. "Ryan's supposed to be in a few of the pictures." With a wink while indicating tables set up off to the side, Morgan told him, "We can sit over there with a few snacks and ogle the guests."

Chuckling, Monty nodded. "Sounds like a plan. There sure do seem to be a lot of good-lookin' guys here."

"Very true," Morgan agreed as he moved behind Monty's chair. Monty turned his head just enough to see that Morgan's attention was riveted to Ryan's retreating form as he said, "None as fine as my hero, though."

Monty chuckled, not bothering to answer. While, objectively, he could look at Ryan and say he was a good-looking guy, he wasn't Monty's type. Monty liked them a little taller—

over six feet—with a trimmer muscular build as opposed to bulky.

In fact, like that guy over there.

As Morgan rolled them toward a table, Monty found his attention riveted on a man who filled out his jeans and sports coat to perfection. His shoulders were wide, his legs were long, and his thick black hair had been pulled into a short tail at his nape, showing off his Native American features. Monty wanted to trace his fingers along the man's firm jawline and down his straight nose before tasting his full lips with his own.

What would those arms feel like wrapped around me? Is he hiding a six-pack underneath that button-down?

"Well, hell, Monty." Morgan chuckled softly as he bent to put his face near Monty's ear. "Someone caught your eye. Wanna tell me who so I can warn you if he's taken? If he's single, I can invite him over."

"Tempting," Monty whispered. "Oh so tempting." Tearing his gaze away from the handsome man, he grinned up at Morgan. "But picking up a trick at a wedding is so cliché."

Morgan scoffed as he straightened. "Who gives a shit." With a shrug of his shoulders, he added, "And who says it'd be a trick, anyway?" Before Monty could quip that *of course it would be a trick*, Morgan started away from him. "I'll grab us some food and drink. Water or iced tea?"

"Iced tea," Monty replied. His buddy knew him well.

Morgan nodded and headed over to get in line at the buffet table.

Monty relaxed in his wheelchair beside the table. Resting his casted arm on his blanket-covered lap, he turned his attention to the happy couple once more. They were still grinning like idiots as the photographer ordered them into different positions.

Their happiness pulled a smile to Monty's lips as he continued to watch. The spectacle allowed him to forget his own troubles for a while. He wondered how people who seemed like such opposites could have ended up together . . . and how could they be so sure, considering Jake couldn't have been more than in his early-to-mid-twenties.

"Well, I hope it works out for them," Monty muttered.

His stomach rumbled softly, reminding him that it'd been several hours since breakfast. He turned his attention back to the buffet, searching for Morgan. It irked the hell out of him that he couldn't walk over there and get his own food and drink.

With his injuries still so new, Monty knew being pushed over the ground would have hurt like hell.

Hmmm . . . thinking about pain.

Monty registered the dull ache in his leg. He pulled out his phone and checked the time. The pain made sense as it was about time for another dose of meds.

To Monty's relief, he spotted Morgan making his way toward him. The man carried a plate in each hand with a bottle of something under each arm. When he reached Monty, Morgan turned, presenting the bottle under his right arm.

Catching on, Monty quickly took the drink, relieving his friend of his burden. The cold bottle chilled his fingers, telling him it'd been in a cooler. He smiled, seeing it was one of his favorite brands of unsweetened tea.

"Thanks." Monty tucked it under his right arm so he could use his left hand to crack the seal as he watched Morgan set the rest of the items on the table. He took a swig, appreciating the way the cool fluid slid down his throat. Licking his lips, Monty eyed the meat and cheese croissant sandwich on his plate. "Is that roast beef?"

"Yep," Morgan replied as he took his own seat. "Knew you'd like that."

"Oh, yeah."

Monty loved roast beef, and he quickly reached for it with

his right hand. A twinge went through his limb. With an annoyed sigh, he lowered his dominant arm back to his lap and grabbed it with his left instead.

"You'll get used to it, Monty," Morgan offered in commiseration.

"Yeah, I know." Monty scoffed. "Just in time for me to be healed up."

Morgan's smile turned wry. "Yep."

After issuing a low chuckle, Monty took a big bite of his sandwich. He moaned softly as he chewed, enjoying the flavors rolling across his taste buds. The meat was succulent, the cheese mild, and there was a hint of tang to whatever the condiment was.

Definitely not just mayo.

Even the croissant was soft with just the right amount of flakiness, with a hint of butter undertone.

Monty quickly chewed, swallowed, and took another big bite. Within minutes, he'd polished off the small sandwich. Grabbing his napkin, he awkwardly wiped his fingertips one-handed. Then he picked up his drink and took a couple of gulps.

"That almost sounded pornographic," Morgan teased, smirking at him.

Grinning broadly at his friend, Monty grabbed a *Dorito*. Before popping it into his mouth, he quipped right back, "As if you know anything about porn. You never watched any."

Morgan shrugged. "Not on purpose, true enough."

"I have, and Morgan's completely right." Upon hearing the deep voice, Monty whipped his head to the right. He nearly choked on the chip he was chewing when he took in the handsome Native American man he'd been ogling earlier. The guy indicated the seat near Monty's wheelchair. "Mind if I join you guys?"

Morgan smiled as he waved toward the chair. "Have a seat, Brian." As the man—Brian—sat, Morgan pointed at Monty.

"This is my buddy, Monty Worshack, and as you heard, he likes to make love to his food."

Monty felt the heat of a blush threaten at the base of his neck, and he ruthlessly fought it back. "Well, who can blame me?" he responded gamely. He indicated the second sandwich that Morgan had provided for him even as his mouth watered for another reason—the sexy man sitting right next to him. "I can never get a sandwich to taste as amazing as when they're professionally done. This is"—he brought his fingers to his lips and kissed them before taking on a fake French accent—"*magnific!*"

To Monty's surprise, Brian narrowed his eyes and swept his gaze over his torso. "*Magnific* is right," he stated boldly before picking up his own croissant-which—turkey from the look of it.

That look burned Monty right down to his toes. His heartrate kicked faster, and he felt the low burn of arousal in his gut. His prick even started to thicken. Except, when Monty shifted in his seat, a spike of pain shot up his leg.

Damn the timing.

"I heard you're a circus performer," Brian commented before taking a bite of his food. "How'd you get into that?"

After swallowing another *Dorito*, Monty replied, "I started gymnastics when I was eight. I loved it and kept at it." He narrowed his eyes and offered Brian a heated smile. "I certainly enjoy how flexible it makes me." Even as Monty caught the spark of arousal that flared in Brian's nearly black eyes, a low throb pulsed through Monty's leg. Grimacing, Monty sighed as he eased his hand under the blanket on his lap so he could rub his leg near the top edge of his cast. "Not now, unfortunately."

"Would it be rude to ask what happened?" Brian asked, his deep voice soft with sympathy. He took a bite of his sandwich and waited patiently, his focus on his face.

Wincing at the memory, Monty quietly answered, "I was

24

practicing a new trick, and the right line of my trapeze broke." He frowned, shaking his head. "The line was new, too. Only a couple of weeks old. I've always inspected my lines meticulously for wear." Pushing the oddness away, Monty met Brian's gaze. "Coupled with a corner of the safety net being down, I'm damn fortunate to only have a broken leg and a few micro-tears in my right wrist." Monty lifted his casted arm. "I'll be out of this in another couple of weeks."

"Damn." Brian shook his head. "I've always admired the nerves of steel people like you must have." His expression turned wry. "I'd never get on one of those things."

Monty chuckled softly. "That's probably a common feeling." Another twinge shot through his body, and he couldn't stop himself from wincing. Monty turned to Morgan and noticed his friend was peering at him with concern. "Uh, I'm due for my next round of pain meds."

"I thought as much," Morgan replied, rising to his feet. "The wedding ceremony started a little later than I'd anticipated."

As Morgan pulled out the bag that had been tucked into the pouch at the back of Monty's wheelchair, he tried to think of something that would distract himself from the rising ebb and flow of pain rolling through him. He focused on Brian and asked, "What about you? What do you do?" Picking up his drink in anticipation of needing it to swallow the pills Morgan would give him, Monty continued, "How do you know the grooms?"

"I'm a police officer," Brian told him, picking up a chip. "I've known Jake for years, even though technically, I'd be considered Carl's friend."

"Oh, you're a detective like him?" Monty questioned.

Brian quickly shook his head. "No. Beat cop." With a wry smile, he added, "I love the variety. Going out on patrol, meeting new people, helping and protecting others." Waggling his brows, Brian grabbed the glass of wine he'd brought over with his plate. "Responding to crime and getting to put away the bad guys."

Monty snickered softly, nodding. "And now who has the nerves of steel?" he teased before sobering quickly. "After all, I imagine you end up getting shot at on occasion, don't you?"

Brian nodded once, his smile turning wry. "Fair enough. Just a different kind of steel, then. And yes," he answered without having to be asked. "I've been shot at more times than I've bothered to count, and yes, I've been hit a couple of times."

Wincing, Monty couldn't imagine purposefully putting his life on the line day in and day out. "Mad respect," he murmured.

"Uh." Morgan looked up from where he'd been rummaging through the bag on his lap. "I can't find your pain meds, Monty."

Monty slowly put down his iced tea. "Uh, really?"

"I'm really sorry." Morgan's lips tightened in a sharp line as he peered toward the wedding party, who were still having their pictures taken. "I'll get the keys from Ryan and take you home." Morgan rose again. "I'll pick him back up later."

"Shit." Monty hated being a bother, but he could already feel sweat beginning to pop out on his temples. "O-Okay. I'm sorry."

"Don't apologize," Morgan ordered as he tucked the bag back into the pocket of Monty's wheelchair. Grumbling, he muttered, "I'm the idiot who left the bottle on your kitchen counter."

"I could take him home," Brian offered, glancing between them. "That way, you don't have to worry about coming all the way back here."

"Why would you do that?" Monty asked in disbelief.

As much fun as it would have been to think it was to enjoy a romp together, Monty knew he was in no shape for that.

Winking, Brian rose. "Protect and serve, remember?" Then he stuffed the rest of his sandwich into his mouth.

Monty glanced between them, seeing Morgan's torn look. His friend obviously wanted to stay.

"You vouch for him, Morgan?" Monty asked, pointedly referring to his safety, even though he couldn't imagine any of Carl's cop buddies not being trustworthy.

Morgan smiled, his tension easing. "Yeah. I vouch for Brian."

Monty nodded once. "Then I accept."

CHAPTER FOUR

Brian hid his amusement upon watching Monty openly vet his trustworthiness. In truth, it was a good move. After all, Monty couldn't defend himself with his injuries . . . if he even had the ability when he was healthy.

Instead, pleasure flooded him upon getting the opportunity to spend a little alone-time with the handsome acrobat.

"I'll call you later this evening, Monty," Morgan told him, gathering the dishes at the table. As the doctor closed the bottle of iced tea, he asked, "Do you want to take this with you?"

Monty reached out while nodding. "Thanks."

After handing it over, Morgan smirked at Brian while sliding the glass of wine Brian had brought to the table toward himself. "You, however, cannot take this with you."

Brian chuckled at the friendly man's antics. "Too bad. It's good."

"It won't go to waste," Morgan teased with a wink. "I'll drink it." Then he sobered. "Unless you have some cooties or germs I should know about."

Shrugging, Brian shook his head. "Naw. I'm healthy." He waved toward the glass he'd barely touched. "Feel free."

While Morgan nodded, Brian moved behind Monty's wheelchair. "Let's get you home so you can start feeling better."

Brian hadn't missed the hints of pain that had caused Monty's eyes to narrow a smidge or the tight lines that had formed around his thin, sensual lips.

Damn. Did I really just think that? I must really need to get laid.

"Thanks," Monty murmured, glancing over his shoulder at him. Then he rested his injured wrist on his right leg while gripping the left handle with the other.

When Brian began easing the chair away from the table, rolling it over the fairly smooth lawn, he still caught the way Monty's breathing hitched and his knuckles whitened.

"Take long slow breaths, Monty," Brian encouraged as he turned the chair and moved it forward. "I'm going to go around the side of the house instead of taking you through it. It'll be quicker and will avoid the stairs." While Monty nodded, Brian focused on a still worried-looking Morgan. "Give my regards to the happy couple."

Morgan nodded, and Brian started them on their way. He did his best to keep his movements steady and sure. Sweeping his focus over the lawn, Brian assessed the ground for levelness.

"H-Have you ever pushed someone in a wheelchair before?" Monty asked softly. His words came out a little tremulous, betraying just how much pain he was in.

"I have," Brian revealed. Figuring Monty could use something to focus on, he told him, "I have a younger brother and a younger sister. When my brother, Cam, was twelve and I was fifteen, he broke his leg and ended up in a wheelchair for a few weeks." Unable to help himself, Brian chuckled a little as he continued, "I used to push him around the house at a run. It was fun, and it cheered him up."

Monty chuckled, flashing a grin over his shoulder at him. "Sounds like you were a good brother."

Feigning offense, Brian gave him a mock scowl. "*Was?* I'm *still* a good brother." He chuckled low in his throat and winked upon seeing Monty's pretty hazel eyes widen in surprise. "I'm also the mean big brother because I like to run background checks on Cam and Sibil's dates."

"Sibil?"

Brian nodded. "My sister. She's five years younger than me." Seeing Monty's brows furrow, he quickly added, "I'm thirty-four."

Monty arched a brow as he glanced over his shoulder at him. With the way his gaze swept over him, Brian felt certain he was being checked out.

"A cop in his prime," Monty mumbled, barely loud enough for him to hear. When he added just as quietly, "And me stuck in this fucking chair. Story of my life," Brian realized the hottie hadn't intended for him to hear.

Hmm . . . he's definitely attracted.

With his lips twitching, Brian eased the wheelchair onto the sidewalk. "My SUV is parked over there." He paused and used one hand to point to an older model vehicle. "I hope you don't mind if I pick you up to put you in the passenger seat," Brian told him, resuming his trek. "That okay with you?"

Monty nodded. "It's fine." With a shrug, he muttered, "Ryan lifted me in and out of Morgan's sedan."

"Okay." Stopping next to his SUV, Brian stuck his hand into his pocket. "Hopefully, this'll be a little more comfortable than a car." Brian hit the unlock button without bothering to pull his keys free of his jacket. Just to see Monty's response, Brian lowered his voice to a husky rumble and teased, "And I'll try to refrain from groping your sexy body *too* much."

Sucking in a sharp breath, Monty lifted his chin to focus on him. "If I wasn't in this wheelchair, I would climb you like a ladder." His hazel eyes darkened, the flecks of green becoming more intense. "And I'd totally rock your world."

Brian smiled hungrily at the other man. "I'd totally let you, Monty."

Swallowing hard as his body reacted to the obvious desire on Monty's face, Brian turned and opened the front passenger door. He inhaled deeply as he adjusted the seat back as far as possible. Refocusing on Monty, he grabbed the blanket that had been draped over his lap and began folding it. He swept his gaze over the way the man's leg cast was mostly straight.

"Maybe the back bench seat would be more comfortable for you?" Brian offered, placing the blanket on the front seat.

Monty looked into the cab and nibbled his bottom lip. With a sigh, he nodded. "Yeah, sorry."

"No need to apologize," Brian countered with a smile, opening the rear door. "Let's get you up here and buckled in."

After setting the brake on the chair, Brian eased one arm behind Monty's back. He gripped Monty's left upper arm and carefully eased him to his right foot as close to the door as possible. He helped Monty pivot, then indicated the handle along the vehicle's upper frame.

Once Monty had grabbed the handle with his left hand, Brian moved to his right side. "Okay. Be careful," he urged, resting his hands on Monty's waist. "We'll slide you up onto the bench seat. Don't hit your cast now."

Monty nodded even as he bit his bottom lip in concentration.

"Pull up on three," Brian instructed while tightening his hold, noticing the trim, firmly muscled waist beneath his hands. *Very nice!* Doing his best to control his desire to rub his thumbs over Monty's lean hipbones, Brian counted down.

When Brian hit three, he lifted, easily hefting the lean, five-foot-nine man. He used a smidge too much force, and Monty's head bumped the roof. With a hiss, Monty settled his butt on the edge of the seat.

"Shit, sorry," Brian quickly apologized, even as he steadied Monty's casted leg so it wouldn't hit the side of the SUV. He stared at Monty, worry filling him when he just sat there for a second, pain etched clearly on his features. "You okay?"

After inhaling deeply, his chest expanding widely, Monty opened his eyes and nodded once. "Still getting used to this."

"How long ago did this happen?" Brian asked, even as he carefully maneuvered Monty into the cabin.

Probably should have asked that before.

"Not quite two weeks," Monty told him, before letting out a deep breath. "I'll be okay. Just give me a sec."

Damn.

Nodding, Brian grabbed the blanket and draped it over Monty's legs.

"Uh." Monty's brows furrowed. "Don't you want me to buckle up?"

Brian winced. "That probably wouldn't be comfortable for you," he admitted. "Just don't tell anyone."

Monty smirked at him. "Yes, Officer."

"Minx," Brian murmured, shaking his head.

"I wish."

Nodding, Brian eased the door closed, not wanting to slam it and rock the injured man. He hurried to the back and tucked the wheelchair inside before climbing behind the wheel. After firing up his SUV, Brian buckled up.

"Okay, where am I going?" Brian asked, peering at his passenger in the rearview mirror.

Opening his eyes, Monty smiled wanly at him. "An address would help, huh?"

"Yep." Brian smirked at the man. When Monty rattled off his address, he whispered under his breath, "Damn."

Brian knew the area. It was on the rim of the valley and full of large, well-appointed homes with impressive-sized lawns and great views of the valley. When Brian was still with Zack, his boyfriend would like to drive through the area and point out all the great homes and share his dream of living there someday.

As a police officer, there was no way Brian would ever be able to accommodate him.

Just one of the reasons Zack left me.

"My grandfather left it to me," Monty murmured, his voice sounding strained. "Pissed off my parents. Glad I was an only child."

Another glance in the rearview mirror showed Monty

slumped against the opposite side door. He had his lips parted, and he panted softly. His brows were furrowed, and there was a gleam of sweat on his pale features.

Shit. I really gotta get him home and comfortable.

"Keep relaxing, Monty," Brian encouraged as he started them on their way. "You'll be home soon."

"Thanks."

Over the roar of his SUV's engine, Brian wondered if he'd imagined Monty's word.

Nearly thirty minutes later, Brian pulled into the driveway of the address Monty had given him. He held in his desire to whistle once more. The beautiful home before him sported deep red siding with stone columns and trim work. The front door had to be an extra-wide, eight-footer with an arched top.

Parking in front of one of the closed bay doors of the three-car garage, Brian wondered where the paved path around the left side led.

"Will you park around back, please?" Monty murmured, peering at him with one partially open eyelid. "My friends had a wheelchair ramp installed on the back deck."

"Sure."

Brian reversed and pulled back a little. Then he turned the wheel and changed directions. A second later, he did his best not to gape. The back was even more impressive than the front.

The pavement led to a tall workshop with a double vehicle door. There were exterior stairs leading up to the second floor, giving the impression of an apartment. The back deck was, in a word, huge. It held a built-in grill with a seating area positioned around a stone, gas-powered fire pit, as well as a hot tub off to the side. An inground pool was nearby with a waterfall feature at one end. A trellis at the end of the yard was to the left of a large flower garden area.

"Damn," Brian whispered.

"My grandma loved spending her time out here." Monty had obviously heard his whispered word. "She used to win awards with her roses."

Although the roses weren't in bloom, Brian still nodded. "I can believe it." He didn't know a damn thing about gardening, but it was obvious someone there did. "Do you share her passion for flowers?"

Monty scoffed. "No. I have a gardener."

Of course, he does.

"Sit tight a sec," Brian ordered before pushing out of his SUV. He quickly fetched the wheelchair, then contemplated the best way to get Monty out. He decided to carefully open the door behind the man's shoulders, using a hand to support him. Then Brian eased him out, one arm around his back while supporting his casted leg with the other.

After settling Monty into the chair, Brian tucked the blanket around him before closing the door.

To Brian's surprise, Monty smirked up at him. "That went way easier than getting in."

"I'm sure I'd get better at it if I had a little more practice."

Shit. Why did I say that? This guy is so far out of my league . . .

"I hope you'll get the chance," was Monty's surprising reply.

Brian just smiled back at the other man and kept his fool mouth shut.

As Brian wheeled Monty up the ramp and to the door, the smaller man pulled a set of keys out of his pocket. He selected one and held it out to him when Brian stopped beside the door. After Brian unlocked and opened it, he gave the ring back to him.

"Will you stop in the kitchen so I can get my meds, please?" Monty requested as Brian pushed him through the door and into a large mudroom. "After that, I'll understand if you want to leave."

Scoffing, Brian shook his head. "I'm not leaving you until

I'm certain you're comfortable," he countered. "You look way too pale to me."

"It'll pass," Monty told him, his side-eyed glance surprisingly shy. "I'll just go lay down and nap for a bit."

"Then I'll help you do that," Brian told him. "Let's go, wheels."

"Wheels?" Monty frowned back at him as Brian pushed him out the door to the left—since the other doorway appeared to lead to a hallway—and into what appeared to be a large pantry. "Because I'm in a wheelchair? Real original, Officer."

Chuckling, Brian admitted, "I used to call my brother that back in the day."

Monty curled his lip in a scowl. "Not sure I wanna be called anything you called your brother."

Brian felt his stomach flutter upon hearing those words. Moving from the pantry to the kitchen, he teased, "How about *Hotwheels* then?"

Turning his head, Monty met his gaze squarely. A hint of desire had replaced some of the pain that had been there before. "Better."

Grinning, Brian paused and peered around the kitchen. With the glass-fronted cabinet doors, he easily spotted the glasses. He grabbed one and headed to the refrigerator, using the door's dispenser to fill it. Then Brian handed it to Monty before grabbing the bottle sitting on the counter. After confirming the contents were painkillers—a heavy dose of *ibuprofen*—Brian opened it as he frowned at the man.

"This all you have?"

Considering Monty's injuries, Brian would have assumed he would have been given something stronger.

Monty nodded. "I don't like how pain meds make me feel," he admitted, his cheeks taking on a slightly pinkish hue. "I don't drink, either."

"Fair enough." Brian wondered if there was a story there, but it wasn't his place to ask. "One or two?"

"One, please." Monty took it and swallowed it quickly. Lowering the glass, he indicated his lap. "Will you put it on my lap, please? I'd like to take it to my bedroom, just in case I need a second one."

Brian complied, placing the bottle on his blanket-covered lap. Then he returned to his position behind Monty and asked huskily, "Where to, *Hotwheels*?"

When, after just a second of hesitation, Monty told him, Brian couldn't help but grin as he wheeled him through the huge estate.

Yep. So damn out of my league.

But that doesn't mean I won't accept a chance to play together if offered.

CHAPTER FIVE

M onty didn't know if he wanted to sneer at Brian's weird endearment — *Hotwheels* — or beg him to join him in bed. It wasn't as if he could do anything anyway. His body flushed hot with arousal, only to have that squashed by a rolling wave of pain from his leg.

As much as Monty wanted to see what Brian could do between the sheets, he knew he didn't have it in him to reciprocate. As it was, as Brian trundled him through his house, he could barely focus enough to tell him which way to go. The place really was way too big for him, but his grandfather had passed it on to him.

As opposed to my father. I'll never give it up.

Sighing, Monty indicated with his casted hand. "This is my room."

"The master's at the end of the hall," Brian commented even as he pushed open the indicated door. "Why this one?"

Monty nodded. "Yep." It wasn't a hard conclusion to come to. After all, the end of the hall boasted French doors. Of course it would be the master. "This was my room whenever I came home from college."

While Monty had never visited his parents when he'd been on breaks from college, he had visited his grandfather. He'd had so many long talks with the aging man. After his grandmother had passed, it hadn't taken Monty much to realize his grandfather considered him all he had left.

While Monty's father hadn't realized it until his grandfather's will had been read, the man had cut him out several years before. His grandfather had been the one to encourage Monty to follow his dreams, no matter where they led. Two weeks after his grandfather's death, Monty had graduated from college with letters of acceptance to several law-focused higher education schools.

Monty hadn't wanted to become a lawyer. With his grandfather alive and well, he'd thought about focusing on gymnastics with an eye for the Olympics. As the man had fallen ill and weakened, Monty had searched for another avenue to enjoy his love for gymnastics.

Monty had run off to join the circus, and other than the occasional battle with his parents about his inheritance, he'd enjoyed his life.

And then this.

"Hey, you still with me, Monty?" Brian rested his hand on his shoulder, teasing his thumb along his neck. "Should I call Morgan?"

"I'm sorry." Monty turned his head and peered over his shoulder at him. "I'm okay. Just tired." Scoffing, he did his best to focus on the handsome man behind him. "Pain seems to take it out of me, which is why I like to make a habit of sleeping through it."

"Gotcha." Brian rounded his chair and knelt beside him. "Comfort is about clothes, not just being pain-free." He waved a hand toward the open doors—one to a closet, the other to a bathroom. "I'd like to assist before putting you to bed." Brian smirked and waggled his black brows playfully.

Monty felt his bladder twinge and nodded once. "Unfortunately, yeah." He grimaced. "I really should pee before lying down."

Brian nodded as he eased the blanket off of Monty's lap, revealing the comfortable shorts it'd been hiding. Considering the full leg cast, he couldn't wear much else. After folding it once and draping it over the bed, Brian reached forward and helped Monty out of his sports coat. Then Brian began unbuttoning Monty's shirt.

With each brush of Brian's fingers against his chest, Monty felt heat spread through his body. It beat out the discomfort . . . almost better than the pain meds. He even felt his nipples bead and his gut warm.

"Where are your sleep shirts?" Brian asked softly, his voice husky, betraying he was just as affected by their interaction. "We'll get you changed. Then I'll help you in the bathroom before helping you settle in."

"Second drawer on the left." Monty indicated the tall boy to the right of the far window. Maybe it was due to the fact that he couldn't really do anything, but Monty couldn't help teasing, "The right has underwear, if you want to rummage."

Brian smirked at Monty over his shoulder. "I just may take you up on that offer." He opened the left drawer and pulled out a soft, striped sleep-shirt. With a wink as he stalked back toward him, Brian added, "But not today."

Monty nodded once, his breath catching in his chest. "O-Okay." His prick even twitched despite the pain still simmering within his body.

"Let's take this off." Brian set the sleep-shirt on the bed, then helped Monty out of the opened button-down he'd worn for the wedding. Pausing, Brian met his gaze while rubbing his fingers along his abdominals. "I hope this isn't too forward, but I really wish I could be doing this under different circumstances."

"Me, too," Monty whispered, unable to keep the words back. Scoffing softly, he smiled up at the man. "Been a long time since I reacted to someone so viscerally." Monty didn't bother trying to hide his body when Brian's eyes narrowed, and the officer roved a hungry gaze over his torso. He'd always worked hard, ate right, and exercised religiously. His job had required it, and Monty knew he looked good. "It's a shame I'm meeting you like this, Brian."

Brian snapped his attention back to Monty's face and smiled at him. His dark eyes glimmered in the overhead light of the bedroom. Even his tanned features seemed to darken with his arousal.

"Well," Brian drawled softly, setting aside the shirt to grab the fresh one. "We've met now, so let's not dwell on what we can't change." His expression shuttered as Brian tugged the shirt over Monty's head. When he could see Brian's face again, Monty spotted the man's relaxed smile as he stated, "While you're in the bathroom, I'll set out your pills and water and turn down your bed."

Before Monty could answer, Brian moved back behind the chair and started wheeling him forward again.

Unable to figure out how to interpret Brian's quick expression changes, Monty remained silent. He felt damn grateful that Jenna kept his bathroom clean—she was a little bit of a germaphobe—when Brian lifted the toilet lid and helped him ease onto it. Just about every surface gleamed, and even the towels looked to have been freshly hung, even though Monty had used them to dry off that morning.

Maybe Jenna really did stop by while I was gone to clean and hang new towels.

When Brian moved toward the door, Monty decided to worry about that later. "I won't be long," he offered.

"Take your time," Brian countered with a shrug. "I'm in no hurry."

Monty began to nod, but a yawn caught him unawares, interrupting.

Brian chuckled and slipped from the room, leaving the door slightly ajar.

With a sigh, Monty focused on the needs of his bladder. Bracing himself with his right foot, he rocked his ass from side to side. As he did that, Monty used his left hand to push his shorts halfway down his thighs.

As Monty tucked his dick down and let go, pissing into the

toilet, he felt silent relief that he hadn't worn any underwear but athletic jocks in damn near two decades. He didn't mind going commando in the least. It certainly made it a hell of a lot easier to go to the bathroom while incapacitated.

Monty finished and grabbed a bit of toilet paper to clean himself up, making sure he hadn't splattered anywhere. Then he leaned sideways, grabbed the newly installed handicap bar, and hauled himself to his feet. Once he was leaning on the wall, Monty slowly pulled his shorts back into place, low on his hips.

With a sigh of relief, Monty made it back into his wheelchair. He reached over and closed the toilet lid. Then he flushed.

Monty thought about trying to wheel himself out of the bathroom, but his body shivered with fatigue. He turned his head instead, and as much as it galled him, he called for Brian.

"Hey." Brian tapped softly at the door even as he swung it open. "You ready for bed, Monty?"

Pasting on a tired smile, Monty nodded. "Who'da thunk a wedding woulda taken it out of me so much?"

"You're in the early stages of healing," Brian countered, gripping the wheelchair and returning him to the bedroom. "You probably did too much." Leaning over him, Brian smiled down at him. "Let me guess, Morgan did warn you not to overdo it."

Shrugging, Monty murmured, "Yeah, but he's also the one who invited me." Wrinkling his nose, he told him, "I think he realized I was feeling a little smothered from my girlfriends."

"Girlfriends?" Brian tensed, surprise etched on his features. "Sorry, I just assumed—"

"Oh, not like that." Monty touched Brian's lips, causing him to fall silent. He scoffed, realizing his slip of the tongue. "Not that kind of girlfriend." Monty rolled his eyes. "I'm totally gay," he assured. Seeing Brian's narrowed eyes and questioning expression, Monty quickly hurried to say, "I meant girlfriends, as in a group of friends who happen to be girls. Donna, Naomi, and Jenna."

Brian tipped his head to the side as his black eyes narrowed a little, his expression turning speculative. "Donna, Naomi, and Jenna." He nodded once, slow and deep, before meeting Monty's gaze again. "Right. I've met Donna but not the others." Scoffing, Brian looked a little sheepish. "Sorry."

Monty snickered as he smiled at him. "No need to apologize." With fatigue and the mild meds swimming through his system, he gave in to his need and reached up to skim the backs of his fingers along Brian's jawline. "Can I at least get a kiss before you leave?"

"Sure, Monty," Brian agreed readily. "Happy to." Then he bent and gripped Monty's hips. "Hands on my shoulders. I'm gonna move you to the bed."

After doing as Brian bid, Monty was lifted from his chair. He strained his legs a little to keep them clear from banging into anything, causing shards of pain to stab through his left leg before Brian eased a hand under his cast to support it. As Brian laid him out on the bed, Monty moaned and a shudder worked through him.

"Damn it, Monty," Brian grumbled. He shook his head as he slid him a little so his head was on the pillow. "You weren't supposed to hurt yourself."

"Sorry," Monty muttered through gritted teeth. "Instinct."

Blowing out a breath, Brian positioned Monty's chair beside the bed before pointing at the full water glass and open bottle of pills. "Just in case. For later." Then he narrowed his eyes as he eased onto the bed beside Monty. "Since I hurt you, it's only right that I help ease that pain."

Monty peered into Brian's dark eyes, allowing his gaze to flicker to his full lips. "What did you have in mind?" He couldn't believe how breathy he sounded, so he decided to chalk it up to the pain.

"First, that kiss you wanted," Brian told him. Resting on his left elbow, he lowered his head. Still holding his gaze, before their lips touched, Brian whispered, "Do I have permission to touch you, Monty?"

"Yes," Monty murmured. "Please."

Brian hummed, a small smile curving his lips.

Then Brian's lips pressed to Monty's, the touch light, exploratory. He adjusted his position as he settled his mouth more firmly against him. When Brian opened and touched his tongue to Monty's bottom lip, he instantly opened to meet the other man's appendage.

Growling softly, Brian deepened the kiss. He thrust his tongue into Monty's mouth, teasing and tasting.

Monty groaned upon his first taste of Brian's deep, masculine flavor. He tasted the tang of the food, a hint of the wine, and something that was all Brian. Wanting more, Monty brushed his tongue alongside the other man's before dipping it into the guy's mouth to do a little exploring of his own.

Brian grunted and shifted a little, threading his fingers into Monty's hair and cradling his skull. His right hand settled on Monty's hip, his fingertips teasing under the edge of his shirt. The hot pads felt like brands on Monty's flesh, causing him to gasp as tingles spread across his stomach and down to his groin. Brian responded by drawing Monty's tongue into his mouth and suckling lightly, and Monty's senses sang.

Lifting his hands, Monty gripped the larger man's shoulders, hanging on for the ride. The move caused Monty's shirt to ride up a little, and he felt Brian's hand slide under completely, palming his stomach. Monty whimpered into the kiss and began to arch, his arousal surging, his dick swollen and aching in his shorts.

Pain sparked up his leg, distracting him.

Monty turned his head, breaking the kiss and letting out a

hiss.

"Relax, Monty," Brian crooned into his ear. "Don't move. Let me do all the work."

As Brian rumbled into his ear, Monty did his best to relax.

"That's it." Brian eased a hand under the waistband of Monty's shorts, scraping his nails along the sensitive skin of his inner thigh. "Mmmm . . . commando. I suspected."

As Brian spoke, he rubbed his nose along Monty's jaw, encouraging him to tip his head back, giving the man more room.

"So responsive," Brian purred, licking and nipping his way down, then back up his neck. "Remember. Let me do all the work."

With goose bumps and tingles erupting through his torso, and his erection throbbing behind the fabric of his shorts, Monty couldn't find the words to ask what Brian had in mind.

A second later, Monty knew.

Brian latched his lips onto the sensitive flesh beneath his ear. At the same time, he wrapped his long fingers around Monty's erection. He squeezed and jacked him in a skilled hold, applying just the right amount of stimulation.

Monty whimpered, fighting his need to rut into Brian's exquisite hold. When Brian swiped a thumb over his crown on an upstroke, his stomach clenched. On the downstroke, Brian rolled his balls before grabbing his prick to jack him once more.

Letting out a groan, Monty felt his balls pull tight. For an instant, he thought about fighting it. Then Brian pinched his frenulum, and he couldn't have stopped it even if he'd tried.

His body erupted with bliss as his orgasm rolled through Monty. He let out a bark of pleasure as a shudder rocked him. The ecstasy of unloading burst after burst of cream—Brian jacking him in a gentler hold and extending his pleasure— beat out the pain in his leg.

Monty floated pleasantly on the endorphins.

Vaguely, Monty registered Brian whispering, "Relax and rest, Monty. I'll clean you up."

Monty tried to murmur his thanks, but he wasn't certain he managed it before he drifted off into blissful sleep.

CHAPTER SIX

Lifting a hand, Brian waved at Cam. His brother had just walked into the diner and was looking around the place. Cam had called him the evening before, asking to meet for lunch.

Brian couldn't remember the last time Cam had asked him to meet for a meal outside their normal monthly catch-up dinners. Worry had filled him even as he'd agreed. Still, Brian had tempered his curiosity, forcing himself to wait to ask questions.

When Cam smiled and waved, Brian relaxed in his seat. He watched his younger brother approach, a grin on his face. Brian noticed his relaxed movements and the twinkle in his eyes that were a deep brown as opposed to the black he'd inherited from their mother.

"Hey, Brian," Cam greeted as he took a seat in the booth across from him. "Thanks for meeting me."

"Always happy to catch up, Cam," Brian replied, wrapping his hands around his cup of coffee and leaning forward on the table. "You look good."

"I am good." Cam smiled at the waitress who appeared at their table. "Cup of coffee, please."

"Of course, sir," she responded with a smile. "I'll go get that and give you a minute to decide." After a glance at Brian's mug, which was half full, she added, "I'll bring the pot to top you off."

"Thanks."

Brian had arrived ten minutes early, having grown tired of

waiting at home. He'd already decided on what he wanted, but he didn't mind waiting while Cam made his selection. Relaxing back in his seat, Brian watched Cam begin checking out the menu.

Unable to help himself, Brian commented, "I'm guessing there's something new with you since you called." He smirked as he met Cam's brown-eyed gaze when he glanced up from perusing the menu. "Something important?"

Cam looked like a deer caught in headlights for just an instant. Then he scoffed and tried to play it off. "I can't ask my big brother for lunch without an ulterior motive?"

Brian snorted. "Some brothers might, but that's not how our family works."

Long ago, Brian's family had fallen into a routine. He and his siblings attended supper at his parents on the second Sunday of the month. The only acceptable reason to miss it was work, illness, or death.

For the most part, that was the only time Brian saw Sibil. She'd ended up a dedicated workaholic after graduating from college with a degree in engineering. Brian met up with Cam for pizza and beer on the third Friday of the month, alternating between each other's houses.

"Okay. Fair enough."

To Brian's surprise, he saw a telltale hint of a blush beginning to creep up Cam's neck.

Huh.

"This couldn't wait," Cam mumbled, returning his attention to the menu. "What are you gettin'?"

"The turkey, ham, and swiss. Cold." When Brian saw Cam's black brows furrow, he explained, "The cold has tomatoes and sprouts on it."

"Oh, right," Cam mused, nodding slowly as he continued to read the menu.

Brian knew that said it all. He loved cold sandwiches loaded with sprouts. While Brian wasn't much of a gardener, he had done quite a bit of research to create a small herb garden. Sprouts was one of the items he'd learned to cultivate. Brian also grew his own tomatoes, cucumbers, baby romaine lettuce, and bell peppers. He hoped to add jalapenos soon. Planting season was coming.

Okay. Maybe I am *quite a gardener, but it took me a decade to get there.*

Thinking of his garden, Brian's thoughts drifted back to the gorgeous garden behind Monty's home. He'd initially asked if Monty gardened to see if they had that in common. Brian had been surprised by how disappointed he'd felt when the cute man had admitted that he didn't.

Good grief. I shouldn't be thinking about him.

The wedding had been over a week before, and Brian had found his mind turning to Monty on many occasions. He wondered how the man was healing. He'd bumped into Ryan at the precinct a few days before, and the detective had thanked him for seeing Monty home so Morgan could stay.

Brian had replied that he'd been happy to help, but he hadn't gathered the courage to ask after him before Ryan had been called away by Carl. Evidently, there'd been a break in one of their cases.

The waitress returned with their coffees and took their orders.

After she'd left, Cam picked up a packet of sugar, opened it, and poured it into the coffee. "So, uh." As he stirred the drink with a spoon, he smiled wryly at Brian. "Poker's this Saturday. You comin'?"

Recently, Brian had started attending monthly poker with Cam and a few of his friends. The first time had been because one of their regulars was sick and another had been called in to work, and they'd ended up needing a fourth, so Cam had begged him. Brian had figured it would be an inconspicuous way to check out his brother's friends—him being the overprotective brother and all.

Brian had ended up really enjoying it. The guys were friendly and welcoming. They'd razzed Brian about being gay, but they'd also razzed each other about the girls they were dating, too. When Cam had asked him to come the next month, Brian had been happy to.

That had been six months before, and Brian had attended every one since.

Did something change?

"I'd planned to," Brian replied slowly. "I have the night off." He'd specifically asked for it. Seeing Cam squinting at his coffee, Brian knew his brother had something on his mind. He reached over and touched his forearm. "Something you want to tell me, but don't know how? Should I not come?"

That would suck. He'd come to like most of the guys, sort of thinking of them as his own friends. He'd been a police officer for so long that his friends from before joining the academy had all faded away long ago. Having non-cop friends was a novelty to him.

"No, no." Cam quickly shook his head. "It's not that." Huffing a sigh, his brother rolled his eyes. "This really shouldn't be so hard."

"Just spit it out, bro," Brian encouraged. "Whatever it is, we'll deal with it."

Cam opened his mouth, closed it again, then heaved a sigh. "Uh, so . . ." He finally met Brian's gaze. "Are you seeing anyone?"

Brian lifted his brows, surprise surging through him. He couldn't remember the last time his brother had asked about his dating life. His mother asked every month, but his siblings certainly had never expressed an interest.

"Uh, no." Even as Brian recalled making out with Monty and jacking him off, he shook his head. He ignored the way his body heated at his memory and told Cam with a wry smile, "Haven't really made time to try finding someone in quite some time."

49

"Since Zack," Cam stated bluntly.

Brian just managed to keep his expression neutral. "Right."

Cam huffed a breath and reached over to grip his wrist. "Sorry about how things ended with that asshat."

Forcing a smile, Brian patted his brother's hand twice before drawing away. "Me, too." He picked up his coffee. Before taking a sip, he stated, "Why do you ask?"

"Because Henry has a crush on you," Cam stated in a rush. He glanced into his coffee for a second before meeting Brian's gaze again. "I think he's going to ask you out on Saturday."

"Oh." Brian stared at Cam in shock. "Really?"

Cam held his gaze while nodding once.

"How do you know?" Shaking his head, Brian rolled his eyes. "Stupid question. He probably asked if you knew if I was dating anyone." When Cam smirked while dipping his chin, Brian barked a laugh. "God. High school much?"

Shrugging, Cam admitted, "A little, but you know how awkward Henry is."

Brian took another sip of his refreshed coffee as he thought about Henry. The man stood about five-foot-ten, was a little pudgy, and wore glasses. He figured if someone looked up accountant in the dictionary, Henry's picture would be right there.

While Brian knew it was stereotypical, Henry looked exactly as one would think from someone who worked in his profession. Brian recalled how Henry had joined them straight from work one poker night, and he'd even been wearing a tie and pocket protector.

I didn't even think those were a thing anymore.

As nice as the guy was, Brian had never felt one iota of attraction to him. "I appreciate the warning." He sighed deeply as he scowled at the table. "This'll make things a little awkward."

Cam winced. "Yeah, you don't want to lead him on, but you don't want to hurt his feelings, either." Then he leaned forward and pinned him with a questioning look. "Unless I'm wrong and you do feel some attraction to him, but you didn't want to act on it because he's a friend from college?"

Brian knew that Cam was two years older than Henry, and they'd shared a number of mathematics classes over the years. After joining the same study group, they'd struck up a friendship. Cam had always had an easy time making friends, and Brian had always assumed he'd taken the awkward guy under his wing to help him out.

"I . . ." Brian tried to imagine himself holding Henry's hand, cradling his jaw, or kissing him. Except, Monty's blond features immediately superimposed over his imaginings, and Brian shook his head. "I really don't feel any attraction to him."

"I figured."

Cam offered him a commiserating smile. He opened his mouth, then snapped it shut again as he leaned back in his seat, his attention sliding to someone behind Brian. A second later, the waitress appeared with their food.

They waited as she set their plates before them, offering *thank you*s in all the right places.

Brian grabbed the ketchup bottle and squirted a large dollop onto his plate next to his pile of fries. His mind reeled with the new knowledge. He really didn't know what to say to his brother other than the obvious.

Picking up a fry, Brian dipped it in the ketchup. "I really do appreciate the warning." He did, too. It would allow him to plan an appropriate response if Henry did indeed ask him out.

"Sure." Cam shrugged. "Warning you was the least I could do."

"Hey, Brian. How are you?"

Looking up, Brian spotted Carl and Ryan standing there.

He smiled at the detectives. "Hey, guys. Doing well." He indicated his brother. "This is my brother, Cam O'Reilly." Then Brian introduced the pair of detectives.

"Hey, nice to meet you both." As Cam shook hands with them, he indicated the table. "Did you just get here? You can join us." With a wicked grin, Cam stated, "I'd love to hear some embarrassing tales about Brian at work."

"Har, har," Brian growled, frowning at his brother. Glancing between the pair, he did offer, "But you're both welcome to join us. I can slide over by Cam."

Carl and Ryan exchanged glances. When Carl refocused on Brian, he grinned. "Sure, thanks."

Brian quickly moved, sliding in beside his brother. Ryan flagged the hostess, letting her know of the seating change. The woman told them she would send their waitress back out right away.

"Thanks for letting us join you," Carl stated as he relaxed in his seat and looked at the menu that Ryan handed him. The other detective had taken them from the hostess and sat next to him. Glancing up, Carl grinned. "Jake and Devon will be sending out *thank you* notes when they get back from their honeymoon, but he sure appreciated that gift card you bought them."

"Who are Jake and Devon?" Cam asked curiously. Then his eyes widened. "Oh, they're the couple that got married the other weekend, right?"

Since Brian had just shoved a fry into his mouth, Carl answered. "Yeah. Jake's my son." The pride in Carl's tone could be heard loud and clear.

"Cool. What did Brian get them for their wedding?" Cam asked, stabbing his fork into his taco salad and mixing the guacamole and sour cream.

"A gift certificate good for a couples massage," Brian told Cam. After a glance at Carl, who nodded imperceptivity, he explained, "Devon was in a car accident years ago, and it messed up his leg. The massage will be good for him, and it'll be a nice thing they can do together."

"Nice." Cam grinned. "I love massages." As he lifted a fork to his mouth, he asked, "Where'd they go on their honeymoon?"

"Africa." Carl chuckled as he shook his head. "Jake's always wanted to go on a safari, and now he's finally getting to."

"Sweet." Cam appeared suitably impressed.

The waitress arrived with two coffees and took the detectives' orders before hurrying off again.

"Thanks again for taking Monty home," Ryan stated, wrapping one hand around the coffee cup. "I know Morgan felt horrible that he'd forgotten his buddy's meds." He smiled warmly as he added, "Heard from Donna that Monty was sleeping like a baby when she arrived to check on him, though. Thanks for putting him to bed."

Brian fought back a blush as he thought about how he'd *put him to bed*. Forcing a smile, and his voice to come out even, he offered, "I'm always happy to help a friend." Unable to help himself, Brian asked, "How's he doing? On the mend?"

"Yep," Ryan confirmed. "Monty'll get the cast off his arm next week, making him much more mobile. In a few weeks, they'll reevaluate his leg to see how it's healing."

"Good." Brian picked up his sandwich. "Glad to hear it."

Cam smirked and gave Brian a speculative side-eyed look. "Sooooo . . . you took a man home and put him to bed?"

Carl snickered as Ryan chuckled low in his throat. "Heard Monty asked about you, too."

"He did?" Brian had received a message from Monty. He'd written the guy's number down, but he hadn't called him. Recalling why, Brian quickly shrugged. "Well, I'm glad he's doing well."

"You could ask him out on a date for this Saturday," Cam stated, straightening in his seat. "You know I can't lie for shit, and I don't like to try." With a grin, his brother told him, "Then I could tell Henry that you couldn't make poker night because you were on a date, and he'd know you're not available."

Brian groaned. As much as he would love to date Monty, he knew it would never work. For one, the guy was rich. And second—

"Ah, no-go, bro," Brian countered, shaking his head. "I, uh, might have snooped after he fell asleep." Holding Cam's gaze, he told him, "I woke his laptop. He's looking for jobs out of state."

Cam immediately understood and nodded. "Ah. Okay."

"What's going on Saturday night?" Ryan asked curiously.

After the pair had explained his problem, Carl offered, "I bet Vince or Trace could set you up with a date for Saturday."

"Uhhh . . ." Brian didn't know how he felt about that. After a second, he lied, "I'm really not interested in a relationship right now."

Ryan and Carl exchanged a look, and Brian didn't think either man was convinced. Still, Ryan reached over and patted him on the upper arm. "Just as friends."

Feeling a little railroaded, Brian nodded. "Okay. Sure."

With a wicked grin, Ryan focused on Cam. "So, this one time, Brian was out on patrol, and—"

"Oh, good grief," Brian grumbled, shaking his head.

CHAPTER SEVEN

"You saw him where?"

Monty did his best to hide his disappointment, but he knew he wasn't completely successful when Naomi's look turned commiserating.

"The *Boar's Head Bar and Grill*," Naomi repeated, tucking a loose strand of her red hair behind her ear. She sat on the recliner to the left of where Monty relaxed on the sofa. Scowling, Naomi grumbled, "What a stupid name. Who came up with it?"

"It's sort of catchy," Monty murmured absently, working through his disappointment. "At least that explains why he never called. He's already dating someone."

Except, why did he make out with me and give me the best damn hand job of my life?

Guess it's really not my business anyway.

"Monty?"

"Hmm?" Monty blinked and turned his attention back to his friend. "What was that?"

"Want me to order pizza for dinner?" Naomi eyed him expectantly.

Monty chuckled softly, recalling how pizza had been their *go to* meal whenever they were getting over an ex. His two-month stint dating a guy named Wayne had been his longest relationship ever. Monty's friends had always lasted far longer.

Considering Monty had always been so busy with training, classes, and friends, he figured a guy putting up with his shitty schedule for two months had been pretty good. He'd stuck with back-room hook-ups after that. Their pizza nights had been to help his girlfriends.

"That's really not necessary for me," Monty told her, smirking at her. "Brian brought me home. That was it." Shrugging, he continued, "He was just being a nice guy."

"Morgan told me about the heated looks Brian was giving you," Naomi countered, disappointment in her tone. "He definitely thought there could have been something between you guys."

"What would be the point?" Monty grumbled, frowning at her. He was getting tired of Naomi pressing him about this. Annoyed, Monty pointed out, "I'm not even sure where I'll end up in six months after finishing rehab."

Narrowing her green eyes, Naomi snarked, "Well, maybe if you had a reason to stick around, you wouldn't leave us again, jackass." Her redhead temper was definitely showing.

Monty groaned softly, barely resisting rolling his eyes. "I'm sorry, Naomi." Forcing a smile, he told her, "You know I didn't *leave you*." He lifted his left hand and made air quotes. "I got a job in a circus. Circuses travel. That's just the way it is."

Naomi nodded, her smile returning. "I know. I'm sorry. I just missed you, is all." Leaning on the arm of her chair, she curled her lip as she added, "And I know it got you away from your dick parents at a really tough time."

Nodding, Monty silently agreed. Once his grandfather's will had been read, his parents had begun the process of contesting the will. At the same time, they'd tried to pressure Monty into handing everything over to them, his father claiming that he was his son, and it should rightfully belong to him. They'd even attempted to break in and steal things, but his caretaker had called the cops, and they'd been arrested. Monty had used that as ammunition to have them banned from his property.

With Monty traveling out of state, it'd been a simple thing to block their calls and force all correspondence to go through his lawyer.

Sitting with Naomi, though, Monty realized he'd missed his friends. The circus environment had been an odd mixture of family and competition. The people there were more frenemies than actual trusted friends. Monty sure had appreciated the invention of products that allowed him to see his friends while chatting instead of them being just a voice over the phone.

Monty stared into Naomi's green eyes and wondered what it would be like to see her whenever he wanted. The same with Jenna, Donna, and Morgan. His best friends were the greatest, and he hadn't realized how badly he'd missed them until they'd begun taking care of him.

"What would I even do here?" Monty murmured the words without conscious thought. Seeing Naomi's wide grin, he quickly added, "I've already started looking at job opportunities. There's nothing based here."

Naomi rolled her eyes, issuing an unladylike snort. "Really?" She waved her hand and looked around the large, comfortable living space. "You own a five-bedroom, six-bathroom house in the *right* neighborhood." It was Naomi's turn to make air quotes. "And it's paid for. You have your inheritance from your grandfather, which you've had your investor's handle."

Monty's friends all knew his financial situation. He'd offered his investor's services to his friends, helping them open accounts so they would all be able to retire comfortably.

"Not to mention, you're the most non-materialistic person I know," Naomi stated with a laugh. "You probably only ever used your circus pay for necessities, so the rest has been invested."

"What's your point?" Monty asked, silently confirming her words.

Naomi laughed again. "You're rich, Monty. You probably don't need to work another day in your life if you don't want to."

"Oh, come on." Monty rolled his eyes. "I'd go bonkers in a week." With a scoff, he added, "I must already be going bonkers just to be talking about this."

Shaking her head, Naomi sobered. "No, you're injured and thinking about life changes. That's normal." The doorbell rang, and she rose to her feet. "And since we all know you hate sitting on your ass, open a gymnastic school or something." As Naomi headed out of the room, obviously going to answer it, she added over her shoulder, "Those parkour and ninja warrior gyms are all the rage right now."

Monty fell silent, his brain whirring. Could he become a business man? Own some kind of gymnastic gym? He wasn't totally sure what parkour or ninja warrior gyms focused on. Monty reached for his laptop, intending to look it up.

"Get out of my way, Naomi, or you'll regret it," a familiar deep voice ordered. "I know Monty is here somewhere."

Grimacing, Monty hated the fissure of fear that coursed down his spine. He didn't like being afraid of his father, but he knew the man could get physical when he didn't get his way. The thump of a body hitting a wall, along with the snarled, "Hey," from Naomi, attested to that fact.

Monty grabbed his cell. For just a second, he was tempted to call Brian. He was a police officer, after all. Except, Monty had no reason to think the man would pick up for him.

Instead, Monty dialed Morgan's number. He kept his fingers crossed that his doctor friend wasn't in surgery or with a patient and could pick up. To his relief, the line connected.

"Just a sec, Monty," Morgan stated. Then his voice quieted

as if he was speaking with someone else. A second later, Morgan spoke into the phone once more. "Hey, Monty. What's up? Is everything okay?"

"Don't think so," Monty answered softly. "My father's here. Can't imagine it's for anything good."

"Do you still have a restraining order against him?" Morgan asked, tension filling his voice.

"Not currently," Monty admitted. "I let it lapse since I was rarely in this state."

Silently, Monty cursed his foolishness. He should have known better than to expect his parents to leave him alone while in town. After all, they'd traveled all the way to Alabama when he was in the hospital.

In truth, Monty was a little surprised it had taken over two weeks for them to show up at his doorstep.

"There you are, Montgomery," Cornelian snarled, stalking into the room. Naomi followed, her face flushed with anger even as worry filled her green eyes. Focusing on Monty, he curled his lips into a sneer. "Are you ready to sign the house and its contents over to your mother and me?" Cornelian crossed his arms over his chest and peered down his nose at him. His hands were clenched into fists threateningly. "We've been more than patient for you to get your head out of your ass and do the right thing."

Monty forced a quiet firmness into his voice as he answered, "The right thing is to honor grandfather's wishes."

"This house and everything in it belongs to me," Cornelian roared, raising his hand and shaking his fist at him. "Better be careful, Montgomery." He narrowed his eyes further as he pointed at his leg. "In your current condition, you could very easily have an . . . accident."

Butterflies bumped in Monty's belly. He knew the threat wasn't an idle one. While he'd never run across any proof, he'd seen it many times over his father's career. One way or another, either his opposition changed their mind and agreed to whatever Cornelian had demanded or they would disappear or become incapacitated in some way.

"That sounded like a threat, Mister Worshack," Naomi stated, resting her hands on her hips. "And we won't let anything happen to Monty."

"If that's the case, you won't always be around." Cornelian's expression turned cold and calculating as he swept his gaze over her. "I can think of a couple of friends who love redheads." His chuckle sounded sinister. "They say their fire is such a . . . turn on. Maybe you'd like to meet them."

The way Cornelian said it, it wasn't a question. Instead, it was a threat.

"You disgust me," Naomi declared, perhaps not realizing when to keep her mouth shut. "Why can't you just stop harassing Monty? This isn't your house, and it never will be."

Cornelian's laughter caused the hairs on Monty's nape to stand on end. "Yes, they'll definitely enjoy spending some quality time with you." He refocused on Monty. "Unless you give me exactly what I want, Montgomery."

"Don't give this asshole anything," Naomi responded hotly, fiery anger replacing her worry. "You get out of here. Now! Before I call the cops."

Ignoring Naomi, Cornelian continued to pin Monty with a creepy, reptilian stare. "Think about what I've said, Montgomery. You wouldn't want something . . . unsettling . . . on your conscience, would you?"

Monty couldn't find his voice as cold dread curled in his gut.

Cornelian's chuckle sounded sinister. "I expect to hear from you by Friday." Then the man turned and strolled out of the room as if he didn't have a care in the world.

Naomi glanced at Monty before following him, perhaps making certain that the man left.

"Monty? You still there?"

Hearing Morgan's voice through the line, Monty realized the call was still open. He sucked in a sharp breath as he rubbed the back of his neck with his left hand. Fear sweat dampened his flesh as he lifted the phone held with the fingertips of his right hand back to his ear.

Monty wasn't even certain when he'd lowered the phone.

"I'm here," Monty whispered.

"As soon as your father started making threats, I used a hospital phone to call Ryan," Morgan told him. "Ryan put in a call for a black and white to stop by."

"May as well cancel that. He's gone now," Monty murmured. "Thanks, though."

No sense in tying up an officer's time when his father was gone already.

Unless maybe it's Brian?

"I also recorded the call," Morgan told him. "I'm going to send a copy to Ryan as soon as we're off the line." His voice turned soothing as he stated, "From what was said, from your father's intonation, I'm sure you'll be able to get the restraining order reinstated."

With a sigh, Monty admitted, "It's not me I'm worried about." His attention strayed to Naomi as she returned to the room. "He threatened my friends."

"All the more reason for the cops to still come," Morgan countered. "Ryan and I will be there as soon as we're done with our shifts."

"Okay."

"See you soon." Then Morgan disconnected the call.

Monty was damn sure that while Cornelian had made vile comments to Naomi, he wouldn't stop with just her. The very idea that his decision to refuse to give his grandfather's legacy to his father would cause harm to come to any of his friends caused his pulse to race and a chilly tremble worked through him. He suddenly found it hard to breathe. He couldn't seem to get enough air into his lungs, and spots danced before his eyes.

"Take a deep breath, Monty," Naomi urged, kneeling beside him. She rubbed his arm while touching his chin. "Open your eyes and focus on me. Everything will be okay."

Forcing open eyelids he hadn't realized he'd closed, Monty obeyed his friend. He peered into Naomi's vibrant green eyes. She stared back at him with a steely gaze.

"Breathe," she ordered again.

Monty inhaled deeply, sucking in a much-needed lungful of air. As he did it a second time, Naomi smiled and nodded. The spots receded from his vision, but he couldn't help the way the tension remained.

"There ya go," Naomi crooned. "That's the way." She continued to rub his arm while lowering her hand to squeeze his. "I don't know why he's decided to go crazy with threats now, but we'll get through it." With a warm smile, Naomi declared, "*We're* your family. Not him. He doesn't deserve anything of yours."

"I don't want you or the others caught in the crosshairs," Monty whispered, fear still riding him hard.

"We'll figure out a way to make certain that won't happen," Naomi stated firmly.

The doorbell rang once more.

Naomi frowned.

"That must be the cops Morgan called," Monty murmured.

With a nod, Naomi jumped to her feet. "Be right back." She hurried from the room.

A moment later, Naomi returned with two officers.

Monty forced down his disappointment that neither of them was Brian.

CHAPTER EIGHT

"Yeah, I heard the recording. Damn, Monty's father's a real piece of work. I don't like the threats he made against Monty and his friends. Will you look into him for me?"

Pausing where he'd been walking down the hall, Brian felt his heart trip in his chest. He turned back to stare at the door to the break room, which was open a crack. He didn't normally have cause to visit the side of the precinct that the detectives worked out of, but he'd been delivering a file to one of them.

Brian recognized Ryan's voice, and he was certain he'd heard him say Monty's name. Unable to help himself, he eased closer, wondering who Ryan was talking to. The answer came soon enough as Chad's soft tenor answered the detective.

"Sure, Ryan," Chad replied as the clink of a spoon on porcelain drifted to Brian. "Send me the father's deets, and I'll dig into him."

"Thanks, Chad," Ryan replied, his tone serious. "And Chad?"

"Yeah?"

"Do it quietly," Ryan warned.

There was a moment of poignant silence followed by Chad's solemn tone. "You really think he'd hurt his own son?"

"From the recording my Morgan sent me, I do."

"Damn, that's messed up," Chad grumbled. "Some people

63

shouldn't be allowed to breed."

Ryan growled softly before muttering, "You won't hear any argument from me."

Shit. Monty's own father is threatening him?

Why would he do that?

Brian felt a rush of confusion mixed with an odd desire to head over to Monty's and get the details. Wracking his brain, he tried to recall anything Monty had told him about his family during their short time together. He couldn't recall much, other than that his grandfather had left Monty the house and his grandmother had been the gardener in the family.

Oh, wait. He did say that he's an only child, and when his grandfather had left Monty the house, it had pissed off his father.

Could that be what this is about?

But why?

Brian had gotten the impression that Monty's grandfather had passed years before.

Why now?

So deep in thought, Brian completely missed hearing the men's footsteps as they approached the door.

When the door was pulled wide, Ryan stood there. He paused in mid-step, his hand still on the side of the door from where he'd obviously been pulling it. Arching one brow, Ryan stared at Brian for a couple of heartbeats.

Ryan shook his head and stepped back. "Sorry, man," he stated with a short laugh. "You startled me. Coming in for coffee?"

Brian quickly shook his head, getting his act together. "Uh, no. No," he replied, taking his own step back so he wasn't in the pair's way. "Just overheard you talking about Monty." Although Brian knew it wasn't any of his business, he couldn't help but ask, "Is everything okay with him?"

After a couple seconds of hesitation, Ryan let go of the door and started through the opening. "No, not really," he told him. Ryan patted Brian on the shoulder once as he passed him. "Guess Monty's had a restraining order out on his father in the past, and now that he's back in town, it's a good idea to renew it."

"Damn," Brian muttered, frowning as he pivoted to keep the detective in sight. He ignored Chad as the computer specialist headed down the hall in the opposite direction. "Monty mentioned his father was pissed about his grandfather leaving the house to him," Brian commented absently. Rubbing the back of his neck, he continued to allow his curiosity to get the better of him. "What all did he say?" When Ryan hesitated again, Brian knew he'd overstepped. He held up his hand and hurriedly told him, "Sorry, Ryan. I shouldn't have asked that. It's not my place."

Nodding once, Ryan opened his mouth, then closed it again. "Well, you're a friend. Part of our group." He rubbed a palm over his bearded jaw before lowering it, all while eyeing him speculatively. After a quick glance around, Ryan eased closer and, in a low tone, told him, "Monty's father wants his house and everything in it, and he's made some really nasty insinuations about hurting Monty or his friends." After another glance around, he returned his focus to Brian, a tick flexing in his jaw as he ground his teeth together. "While he didn't say it, that may include my Morgan, so we've warned his friends to be careful. We're trying to get the restraining order written in such a way that he has to stay away from not only Monty, but the other four as well."

From Ryan's tight tone and words, Brian realized this was hitting a little too close to home for the detective. When he and Morgan had first met several years before, Morgan had been targeted by a stalker who was killing off guys she'd deemed as competition, even though Morgan had always been an out and proud gay man. Unfortunately, that didn't mean shit to someone who was delusional, and she'd finally tried to kidnap Morgan and kill Ryan in the process. Fortunately, it hadn't worked, and Ryan had saved his man.

This situation was probably bringing back all sorts of feelings in the detective.

Hell, if Brian was in a relationship and someone threatened his man, even vaguely, Brian knew he would be up in arms, too.

"I'm sorry, man," Brian muttered, scowling as he shook his head, trying to think up something appropriate to say. "That's messed up."

Ryan's nostrils flared as he sucked in a sharp breath. After blowing it out through pursed lips, he muttered, "Yeah." Stepping back, Ryan stated, "Anyway, whenever you see Monty, keep your eyes peeled and your ears open."

Before Brian could wrap his brain around that comment, Ryan turned and headed toward his department.

Brian shook his head as he turned and did the same, all the while wondering why Ryan thought he would ever see Brian again.

Sitting on his sofa, a frozen dinner resting on the coffee table before him, Brian stared at the unappetizing meal. The chicken and dumplings had sounded good when he'd popped it in the microwave. Except, as Brian had watched the food go round and round, his thoughts had turned to Monty, and he wondered what the man was eating for dinner that evening.

Is he safe?

Has anything happened to him?

It had been three days since Brian had had his run-in with Ryan.

Whenever Brian hadn't been focused on something, thoughts of the pretty acrobat would invade his mind. He'd recalled the feel of his smooth, firm skin beneath his palms, the taste of his mouth against his own, and the weight of his erection in his hand. The way the man responded to Brian had been such an aphrodisiac that he'd almost come when Monty had.

With a deep sigh, Brian leaned forward and picked up his fork. He twirled it between his fingers as he stared at the meal without really seeing it. Brian didn't make it a habit of lying to himself, and he knew he wanted a repeat performance with Monty.

And maybe more, if he's up to it.

Except, Brian worried he would become too invested. That was why he hadn't returned Monty's call when the man had left him a message. Brian realized he could come to like the man way too much.

Brian had been nosy as hell on his way out the door. He'd spotted the laptop on the table in a spot that didn't have a chair in front of it. Realizing that Monty must have been using it, Brian had woken the device.

There hadn't been a screen asking for a password. Instead, the laptop had flashed right to what Monty had been looking at last. That had been an advertisement for a location in Vegas looking for an aerial silk performer.

Brian's disappointment had hit him damn hard, killing the boner he'd still been sporting after putting Monty to bed.

With a sigh, Brian swiped his fork through the chicken and dumplings. He scooped out a dollop and shoved it into his mouth. Brian grimaced as he chewed and swallowed.

"Yeah, no," Brian muttered, rising from his seat. While the dish wasn't bad, he wouldn't call it good, either. "Maybe with some salt and pepper."

Picking up the plastic bowl it'd come in, Brian headed to his dining room where the salt and pepper shakers rested on the table. As he chose one to sprinkle onto the food, he paused. Once again, Brian wondered what Monty was eating.

And is he safe?

Brian growled under his breath as he set everything down.

Pulling out his phone, he woke the device. He hesitated with his thumb over Monty's number.

To call or not to call?

Would Monty even pick up?

After all, I'm the one that didn't call him back . . . and this is a damn personal matter. If Monty does answer, would it be rude of me to ask about this?

Brian continued to hesitate, his mind skipping from one thought to another. He couldn't remember the last time he'd been so uncertain.

Or would seeing him in person be the better choice?

That way, I can see for myself that he's okay.

Blowing out a breath, Brian shoved his phone back into the holder on his belt. With his mind made up, he headed for the side hall that led to the garage door. Brian grabbed a jacket from a hook and quickly shrugged it on before swapping out his house shoes for a pair of trainers.

Brian grabbed his SUV's keys from a hook and headed into the garage. After climbing behind the wheel, he pushed the button attached to his visor. He heard the bay door behind him begin to open as he fired up his vehicle.

As Brian pulled out of his garage, he felt his stomach grumble, reminding him of his discarded food. He had no desire to show up at Monty's while hungry. That was just rude.

With that thought in mind, Brian paused in his driveway long enough to order a pizza from his favorite pie place. Instead of the hot wings he normally ordered, he chose their boneless option, thinking that would be easier for Monty to handle with a cast on his wrist. Brian added cheesy breadsticks, and at the last minute, he spotted their offered drinks. Recalling Monty's beverage of choice at the wedding, he chose a two-liter of iced tea.

After paying for his order with his debit card, Brian placed his phone in the cupholder and headed on his way.

Forty minutes later, the smell of the food causing his stomach to grumble even more loudly, Brian pulled up to Monty's home. He gave in to the urge to whistle under his breath. The large, two-story place really was absolutely gorgeous with its stone pillars and shaker-covered dormers over the second-story windows.

Brian had almost given himself a complete tour of the place but had managed to keep his nosiness contained to the main floor — barely. Even that had reminded him that Monty was so damn out of his league. There had been a bedroom and bathroom suite off the kitchen, which obviously would have been used by a cook or housekeeper. The study had held a number of heavy oak bookshelves, which were filled with a variety of books — from poetry to law to leatherbound classics.

It hadn't taken a genius for Brian to realize that Monty's grandfather had made his living by being a lawyer, and considering the home, he'd been a good one.

Pushing those thoughts aside, Brian exited his SUV. He rounded it and opened the front passenger door. After collecting the boxes in one hand, he grabbed the two-liter in the other, and used his elbow to shut his door.

Brian stared at the front door for a few seconds before shaking his head and making his way toward it. The cement walk had wood-chipped beds on either side with a number of carefully tended plants and shrubs. There were two steps up to the front patio, and Brian understood why they'd put the ramp onto the back deck. They would have really messed up the front aesthetics.

After a glance over the huge, arched, eight-foot door, Brian spotted the doorbell and rang it. He stepped back a couple of paces and waited. Brian felt his stomach clench as if butterflies bounced within, and he barely resisted rolling his eyes.

Good grief. I'm just checking on a friend. That's all.

With that thought firmly in mind, Brian listened to tumblers click, telling him that someone was unlocking the door.

69

He glanced over the large door again and just managed to keep back his frown. There didn't appear to be a peep hole on the thing.

Hopefully Monty has a hidden camera of some kind to verify who's at the door before he opens it.

Except, when the door opened, it wasn't Monty. A slender woman with medium-brown skin, her black hair piled on top of her head in an impressive number of braids, stared at him. Her dark-brown-eyed gaze glanced from his face to the food he held and back to his face.

"Uh, we didn't order anything," she stated as she began to close the door again. "You must have the wrong house."

Realizing her misunderstanding, Brian quickly tucked the two-liter under the arm holding the boxes. "Oh, I'm not a delivery guy," he claimed, holding out his free hand. "I'm Brian. Brian O'Reilly. A friend of Monty's." *Well, sort of.* "You must be either Naomi or Jenna."

"You're Brian?" she asked as she stepped forward to take his hand.

"I am," Brian confirmed, giving her hand a light shake before releasing her. Indicating the food, he offered her a wry smile. "I thought I'd drop by and check on Monty. Didn't realize he'd have someone here already."

Although I probably should have.

The woman stared at him for a few seconds with narrowed eyes, and Brian sort of felt like a bug under a microscope. He barely resisted shifting from foot to foot in unease. Brian called on all his police training to keep his smile in place and his body loose and confident.

"Jenna, who's at the door?" Monty called from somewhere inside, telling Brian which of his friend the woman was.

Jenna blinked as if coming out of a trance of her own. Even as she turned her head and called out, "It's Brian," she never took her attention off of him.

"Brian?" Monty sounded shocked. "What?"

Yeah, I definitely surprised him.

Mentally, Brian winced.

Maybe I should have called, after all.

"Yeah," Jenna confirmed. "So he says."

Monty rolled into view, fifteen feet behind Jenna. "Brian," he repeated, staring at him in obvious disbelief. "Hi."

"Hi, Monty," Brian rumbled, unable to control the way his voice deepened.

Brian couldn't help sweeping his gaze over Monty, taking in his lean torso covered in a tight t-shirt. His blond hair appeared rumpled, as if he'd just tumbled from bed. Brian felt his prick thicken in his jeans, and his mouth watered for a new reason. The man looked fucking edible.

"He brought pizza," Jenna stated, breaking their stare-down. She glanced between them, her full lips curving into a wry smile. There was definite amusement in her tone when she asked, "Should I let him in? Or just grab the boxes and slam the door in his face?"

Brian held his breath upon hearing those words. He snapped his attention back to Monty and spotted the slight flush filling his cheeks.

Shit. He obviously told them something about me, and they must not think much of me . . .

After clearing his throat, Monty softly murmured, "Let him in."

Relief flooded Brian as Jenna opened the door wider and beckoned him forward.

CHAPTER NINE

A healthy dose of shock mixed with disbelief flooded Monty's system. He sure as hell hadn't expected Brian to show up at his door. After all, the man hadn't even been bothered enough to return his call.

So . . . what's he doing here?

Only one way to find out.

After telling Jenna to let him in, Monty carefully turned his chair and started toward the back of the house. "Come into the kitchen with those," Monty ordered, leading the way.

While Monty couldn't push his wheelchair very fast with his casted wrist, he could do it. He was so looking forward to his doctor's appointment the following Tuesday. The wrist cast would be removed, and his tendons evaluated.

Can hardly wait.

Once in the dining room, Monty turned and watched Brian place the boxes on the counter. He recognized the logo on the side of the box as one he'd always really enjoyed, and his mouth watered in anticipation. On second thought, that could have been caused by the delicious aromas filling the room.

Brian turned to face him and opened his mouth. Before he could say anything, the man's stomach grumbled loud enough for Monty to hear it. Grimacing, Brian peered to the right, and if Monty didn't miss his guess, he spotted a hint of color creeping into the man's cheeks. Although, it was nearly hidden by his naturally bronzed complexion.

Shaking his head, Brian murmured, "Sorry about that."

"I'll get the paper plates," Jenna claimed, moving past

them into the kitchen. "The glasses are in the cupboard to your left, Brian."

"Will you join us?" Monty asked as he watched Brian turn to where Jenna had indicated. "You did bring the pizza, after all." When Brian looked at him over his shoulder, Monty smirked and added, "And it sounds like you could use a little of it."

"Yeah, if you don't mind," Brian replied, his smile appearing a bit wry. "I'd hoped to, anyway."

"I'd, uh, I'd like that," Monty admitted, fighting back a blush at his own admission. After clearing his throat, he focused on the boxes. "So, what did you bring?" Then Monty noticed the two-liter wasn't soda. "Oh." Pleasure filled him when he read the label. "You brought iced tea."

Brian nodded, setting three glasses on the counter. "I did. Noticed that's what you were drinking at the reception."

"Thank you." Monty smiled at Brian. It felt as if something in his chest fluttered at the man's thoughtfulness. "I really do appreciate it."

"You're welcome," Brian rumbled before opening the two-liter. After clearing his throat, he stated, "So, uh, not knowing what kind of pizza you liked" — he paused to fill the first glass before refocusing on Monty — "and knowing you were eating roast beef at the reception, telling me you're not a vegetarian" — Brian smirked and focused on filling the second glass — "I played it safe and brought a three-meat with extra cheese."

Monty hummed appreciatively, and his stomach did its own growling.

Brian grinned at him. "Sounds like you approve."

"Very much," Monty confirmed.

When Brian lifted the bottle to fill the third glass, Jenna set a stack of paper plates on the counter and ordered, "Oh, no. Don't fill that." She opened the top box and hummed. "Yum. Cheesy bread." Jenna reached in and pulled a stick out and set it on a plate. "You're gonna be here for a while, right, Brian?"

"Uh, y-yeah," Brian replied, glancing between them. He focused on Monty. "If that's okay with you, Monty."

"Oh, good," Jenna cut in, not waiting for an answer. "I just remembered I have laundry to finish."

"Laundry?" Monty asked, growing suspicious.

"Mmm-hmmm," Jenna responded, opening the second smaller box. "Oooo, nice. Boneless hot wings." As she plucked a couple of those and placed them on her plate, she stated, "I have an appointment to show a house tomorrow, and I forgot the shirt I wanted to wear isn't clean." With a shrug, Jenna continued, "So . . . gotta go wash it." As Jenna helped herself to a couple of slices of pizza, placing them on her plate, too, she told them, "So, I'm gonna run." With a not-so-innocent smile—Monty knew her way too well—she focused on Brian. "Heard you're a trustworthy police officer, so I don't mind leaving him with you. You'll get him to bed, right?" Then Jenna's innocent look fled to be replaced by a smirk. "You've already done it once, after all."

Without missing a beat, Jenna picked up her plate and rounded the counter. "Okay, then." She bent and pecked a kiss to Monty's cheek.

"What the hell are you doing?" Monty hissed.

Jenna winked, whispering back, "As if you didn't know." Straightening, she headed toward the front of the house. "You guys have a great night. I'm gonna grab my purse and jacket and let myself out." Jenna looked over her shoulder and grinned. "Don't worry. I'll lock up after myself. Enjoy your meal."

Just that fast, Jenna was out of sight.

Monty focused on Brian, trying to gauge the officer's reaction to Jenna's subtle as a wrecking ball matchmaking. Brian was staring at where Jenna had disappeared, an inscrutable look on his face. His black brows were furrowed just a little, and his dark eyes had narrowed.

How embarrassing.

The sound of the front door closing caused Brian to inhale quickly. The man snapped his attention to Monty. He swallowed, his Adam's apple bobbing, drawing Brian's attention to the knob.

Monty wondered what Brian's skin would taste like if he were to suck on it.

"Uh, I didn't mean to run your friend off," Brian murmured, placing the cap back on the tea. Then he scoffed softly before peering at Monty out of the corner of his eye. "Although, she's not subtle, is she?"

"You didn't run her off," Monty assured. With a roll of his eyes, he added, "And no. No, she's not."

Turning to rest his butt against the counter, Brian shoved his hands into his pockets. "You told her about me." Tilting his head just a little, he added, "Us. About . . . what we did together."

"No, not exactly," Monty countered, shaking his head. "I don't discuss specifics of my sex life with my friends."

Brian nodded once. "Okay." Turning back to the counter, he grabbed the paper plates. "But she did recognize my name, though." As Brian began to move everything to the table, he scoffed. "Hell, she even threatened to take the food and send me on my way."

Monty grimaced. "Yeah. Yeah, she did do that." He rolled to the table, watching as Brian set a paper plate in front of him. "And it's because I did mention you to her and Naomi both." With a shrug, Monty stated, "How could I not when you're the one who drove me home after the wedding?"

"Fair enough," Brian commented, placing the box with the chicken bites to Monty's left. There were a couple of sauce cups inside, and he took a moment to peel open each — one ranch and one barbeque. "Where are your forks?"

"Uh, I'll get them," Monty offered, reaching for his wheels.

"No, stay and relax," Brian encouraged, resting his hand on Monty's shoulder. "Just tell me."

Fighting back a shiver upon feeling Brian's big hand warm Monty's flesh through the thin fabric of his shirt, Monty pointed. "Uh, top drawer to the left of the stove."

After squeezing his shoulder lightly, Brian moved away. "Help yourself, Monty," he encouraged. "I plan to." With a shrug, Brian admitted, "I'm hungry. I hope I brought enough." Monty noticed the way his dark brows had furrowed as he returned from retrieving a couple of forks. "Maybe I should have gotten two pizzas. Didn't think about you already having, uh, help."

"I imagine this'll do us just fine," Monty assured, smiling at Brian as he took the seat next to him. "My appetite still isn't huge, yet, and I don't normally eat this many carbs. Thanks for the treat."

Brian nodded. "You're welcome." Pointing at the pizza, he asked, "How many slices?"

"Two, please," Monty answered, picking up the fork.

Using his own fork and thumb, Brian moved two slices to Monty's plate. Monty barely paid attention as Brian added a cheesy breadstick to his plate, too. He was too busy stabbing his fork into a boneless chicken wing and dipping it into the ranch sauce. Lifting his fork to his mouth, Monty bit the piece of breaded chicken in half.

The spicy hotness exploded across his tongue, tempered by the cool ranch dip. The succulent chicken mixed with the light dressing perfectly. The combination of flavors drew a hum of approval from him, and he quickly chewed and swallowed so he could stuff the rest of it into his mouth.

Brian's soft chuckle drew Monty's attention to the man next to him. Out of the corner of his eye, he watched Brian take a big bite of his pizza. A bit of sauce oozed off the side of the slice and clung to the corner of Brian's bottom lip.

Monty had to drag his gaze away, so very tempted to try to lean over and lick it off with his tongue. His prick began to plump at the idea. Swallowing his bite of food, Monty reached for his glass of iced tea.

After taking several swallows of the tasty, slightly-bitter goodness, Monty managed to get himself a bit under control. He knew they had fantastic chemistry together, but since Brian hadn't returned his call, Monty couldn't figure out what the man was doing there. Never one to shy away from asking for answers, Monty set his fork down and picked up the breadstick.

After taking a bite of the cheesy, doughy goodness, Monty turned and focused on Brian. He chewed and swallowed, taking his time, while watching the larger man polish off his piece of pizza. Catching Brian's eyes, Monty cocked his head.

"What are you doing here, Brian?" Monty asked bluntly. When the other man's brows furrowed a little, a look of confusion on his face, Monty sighed and used the half-eaten breadstick to indicate the spread before them. "As grateful as I am for the comfort food, why did you come? You didn't even return my phone call." Monty did his best to keep the hurt from his voice, hating that he wasn't completely successful. His frustration rose with his failure, and he grumbled, "We made out, you jacked me off, blew off my call, went on a date with someone else, and now you're here bringing me pizza. What the hell, man? Are you trying to cheat on that guy with me?" Shaking his head, Monty scowled at him. "Because I don't wanna be that guy."

"I'm sorry for the mixed signals, Monty," Brian told him softly. Picking up the next piece of pizza on his plate, he stared at it, and Monty allowed the silence to lengthen and took another bite of his breadstick. With a sigh, Brian stated firmly, "I'm not trying to use you to cheat on that guy I went out with on Saturday." Cutting a side-eyed look Monty's way, Brian added, "Although, I'm not certain how you knew about that, anyway."

"Naomi and Morgan picked up take-out from the *Boar's Head* and brought it to me for dinner Saturday night," Monty explained, although why he felt the need, he wasn't certain. "Ryan was working, so they hung out with me. Morgan recognized you."

Brian nodded once. "The man I was with, Andrew, we were set up by Vincent and Trace. He's one of their firefighter buddies."

"Blind date?" Monty asked, trying to hide his disappointment.

So, Brian is open to dating. He's just not open to dating me.

When Brian nodded, Monty felt as if his heart squeezed uncomfortably in his chest.

Shit.

"Sort of," Brian amended. "The guys were upfront that I needed someone to go out with that evening, but just as friends."

"Why just as friends?" Confusion filled Monty. "If you're not looking for a relationship, why go on a date?"

"To get out of getting asked out by a guy I play poker with."

Monty shook his head, processing that. "I'm so confused," he admitted before popping the last of the breadstick into his mouth.

The man truly wasn't making any sense.

After swallowing his bite of pizza, Brian explained about his brother's warning of Henry's interest. He shared how he and Cam both knew his brother couldn't lie for shit. Due to that, they'd set up a plausible situation that would dissuade Henry's interest that Cam didn't have to lie about.

"Okay," Monty murmured, understanding the reason, even though it hurt when his message had clearly stated he hoped to see Brian again. Brian obviously hadn't wanted to, which left—"What are you doing here, Brian? Why bring me a meal?"

Lowering the piece of pizza to his plate, Brian admitted, "A few days ago, I overheard Ryan talking about your father threatening you." He turned concern-filled dark eyes on Monty. "I was worried about you. I wanted to make certain you were okay."

Monty's gut churned, and he worried he wouldn't be able to keep down the food he'd just eaten.

"Great. So you pitied me." Scoffing, Monty shook his head. *Isn't that just my luck.*

"Well, now you've seen I'm fine." Pushing away from the table, Monty stated, "I'll show you to the door."

CHAPTER TEN

*S*on *of a bitch! What the hell?*

Brian bit back a growl as he rose from his chair so swiftly he had to grab the back of it to keep it from crashing to the floor. Rushing after Monty, he grabbed the handles of the wheelchair, jerking it to a stop. He grimaced, feeling a measure of contriteness upon hearing Monty's hiss of pain at being jolted.

"Sorry," Brian muttered as he stared down into Monty's upturned face. He was almost distracted by the angry flush filling the guy's cheeks, but the accusation in his eyes had Brian quickly banking his desire to swoop down and capture the man's lips. Instead, Brian quickly stated, "I'll give you this one pass because we don't know each other." When Monty's pretty hazel eyes narrowed further, he began rounding the chair, still holding it in place, as he bent and got into the other man's face. "I do not now, nor have I ever, pitied you. I don't know why the fuck that idea popped into your head, but it's not true, so don't put words in my mouth."

Monty's nostrils flared as he breathed deeply, his lean torso expanding and contracting. A muscle ticked in his jaw as he stared up at Brian. When Monty flicked his gaze from Brian's eyes to his lips and back again, Brian's own breath caught in his chest.

Shit. What is it about this guy?

Straightening slowly, Brian gathered every ounce of self-control he possessed. Monty was still in a wheelchair, still in a couple of casts, and still in no condition for Brian to jump his bones. Plus, Monty still intended to leave.

Keep it in the friend zone.

"Let's go back to the table and finish our meal," Brian stated, moving back to the table, leaving Monty there to decide. "Then we can relax and watch a movie or something. I did tell Jenna I'd stay a while."

Brian had returned to his chair and taken a big bite of pizza—it really was good, and he really was still hungry—before Monty must have come to a decision. He slowly turned his wheelchair and returned to his spot at the table. Picking up his fork, Monty stabbed at another boneless hot wing bite.

Neither of them bothered to speak as they focused on their food, and the tension remained thick in the air.

Doing his best to ignore it, Brian added a third slice of pizza to his plate before helping himself to half a dozen chicken bites, leaving the rest for Monty. He snagged two cheese bread sticks. Leaving one on his plate, Brian dipped the end of the second one into the ranch before taking a big bite of it, humming with pleasure.

"Hey," Monty murmured, finally breaking the silence. "That's for the hot wing bites."

Brian smirked as he chewed. Using his peripheral vision, he flipped the cheese stick in his hand, then dipped the unbitten end into the ranch again. The outraged expression on Monty's face drew a low chuckle from him.

"And now you're double dipping!"

Enjoying the playfully aghast tone, Brian claimed, "I flipped it around and used the clean end." He smirked, adding, "Besides, you've let me have my tongue down your throat, so I don't think you have room to talk."

Monty's mirth faded, and a thoughtful expression took over his features. "We have chemistry, you and I," he pointed out softly. Lifting pizza to his lips, but before he took a bite, Monty added, "Is it because you had to do all the work last time? Because, you know it wouldn't always be like that."

Chewing the last bite of the bread, Brian realized he needed to explain himself. "Yes, we have chemistry," he agreed. Scoffing softly, he took in the hot man sitting beside him. Even a little pale, probably due to pain caused from his injuries, Monty was a sexy man. "And I find you so damn sexy, Monty. Don't think that I don't." When Monty opened his mouth, probably to question him, Brian held up a hand to stall his words. "I was nosy and woke your laptop. I know you're already checking the job market for after you're healed." Brian thought it was a wise decision. Planning ahead would give a healing person that extra push to keep working hard to regain their strength. "But you're looking out of state." With a shrug and a wry smile, Brian admitted, "I'm not prepared to put myself out there for a guy that could ultimately . . . leave the state."

"What if I wasn't planning to leave the state?" Monty countered softly.

Brian felt his heartrate pick up at those words. Hope flared within him. Just as quickly, he remembered Zack, recalling the words in his *Dear John* letter.

With a smile, Brian reached over and squeezed Monty's wrist. "As much as I'd love to take you up on that, I don't think it's fair to put you in that sort of position. Trying to stay for a possible relationship" — seeing the way Monty's eyes widened just a little, Brian hurriedly explained — "and yes, a relationship would be what I want from a partner." Brian paused a moment, trying to return his thoughts to his original line of thinking. After a few seconds, Brian continued, "You don't know me, and I don't know you. I'm a police officer, and you can ask anyone. It takes a certain kind of person to be the spouse or partner of a cop." Not wanting to think Brian was insulting Monty, he shrugged and stated, "Are you that type of person? I have no idea, but I don't want you trying to build a life around this area just to try something with me and have it fall apart when you realize you can't handle those kinds of stresses." Realizing how condescending that might sound, Brian quickly told him, "I had a guy try it before. Zack. We ended up living together for a couple of years before he cheated on me, several times, and took off because he couldn't handle it. Now, maybe I'm not being fair to you, but — " Brian paused again, uncertain what to say.

"But you're not ready to take that risk for a guy who's only in the area because he's forced back here to heal from an injury," Monty whispered, finishing the thought for him.

Brian dipped his chin in a nod, glad Monty understood. "Yeah," he whispered. Shrugging, he added, "I'm sorry."

Monty hummed, his lips curving into a small smile. "At least you're honest. I can respect that." Grabbing his iced tea, he finished the glass and returned it to the table. "So thank you for dinner." Smiling at him, Monty added, "And for worrying about me."

Nodding, Brian told him, "If you need me, I'll help in any way I can." He hesitated a second, then asked, "Would it be too invasive to ask what's going on with your father, past and present, that a restraining order is necessary?"

Arching one brow, Monty stated, "I thought you knew, and that's why you came rushing over."

"Not really," Brian admitted. "I overhead Ryan asking one of our tech specialists to look into your father. Then he told me that you'd been threatened, as had your friends, but not specifics."

"Ryan's looking into my father?" Monty asked, sounding surprised. "Why?"

Picking up the two-liter, Brian began refilling Monty's glass as he told him, "With Morgan being one of your best friends, that puts Ryan on high alert, being his partner and all." He topped off his own before returning it to the table. "Ryan'll cover all his bases to keep his man safe." Returning his attention to Monty, Brian admitted, "Don't take this the wrong way, but helping you is just sort of a side bonus."

Monty scoffed as he rolled his eyes. "Okay. Well." He shrugged. "I'll take it." Sobering, Monty furrowed his brows as he shook his head. "My father won't be pleased if he catches wind that he's being investigated."

"Ryan did tell Chad to tread softly," Brian assured before popping the last of his chicken into his mouth. Around his mouthful, he muttered, "Damn. I'm full but I couldn't let it go to waste."

Grabbing a napkin, Monty nodded. "Me, too." He seemed to be sweeping his gaze over the table, and his expression turned thoughtful. "We did manage to demolish most of it, though."

"Yup." Brian rose from his seat and checked out the remains — one slice of pizza, four hot wing bites, and three breadsticks. "I think I can fit everything into the hot wing bite carton if you don't mind them touching."

"God, no." Monty stared at him with wide eyes. "You can't have your food touching." He shook his head as he stared at him askance. "That'll contaminate the flavors."

Brian opened his mouth, then shut it again. Looking at everything, he murmured, "Ooookay. I can put the pizza slice on your plate, and —"

Monty barked a laugh, redrawing Brian's attention. The man was grinning from ear to ear, his hazel eyes twinkling with mirth as he continued to chuckle. He even had his good arm wrapped around his torso as his body shook.

"Oh, my god!" Monty cried between laughs. "The look on your face."

Realizing he'd been had, Brian growled at the laughing man. "You little shit," he grumbled, but Monty's laughter was infectious. Brian couldn't help but chuckle, too, as he shook his head. "Knew you'd be a handful."

The words were out of Brian's mouth before he could think better of them.

"Yeah," Monty murmured softly, his chuckles slowing. "I figure I would be." Then he cleared his throat and grabbed the pizza slice. "So, yeah. Everything together is fine." Monty eased it next to the chicken bites, pushing them over a little.

Brian swallowed hard, doing his best to ignore the way his half-hard prick threatened to fill the rest of the way. A happy, laughing Monty was just too stunning for words. Even having explained why Brian wasn't going to pursue anything with Monty didn't stop his body from reacting to the handsome man.

Using his fork, Brian peeled the remaining cheesy bread from the paper liner.

Monty grabbed them and placed them on top of the rest of the food.

As Brian began gathering the garbage into a pile, Monty closed the container.

"I'm, uh, I'm going to go to the bathroom before we watch that movie," Monty told him. For some reason, his cheeks started to darken. The reason why became clear when Monty muttered, "It'll take me a few minutes. Um, feel free to pick out a movie to watch."

Brian nodded. "Sure." Then he glanced around the expansive space as Monty began turning his chair to wheel himself away. "Uh, where are we watching this movie?" When Monty looked at him over his shoulder, Brian shrugged and admitted, "I snooped a bit a few weeks ago, and there are a couple of different places with TVs down here."

Monty snorted, and a smile curved his lips. Pointing to the left, he told him, "Down that hall and on the right is a den that I find the most comfortable." Tapping his wheel, he added, "Easiest for me to maneuver, too."

Recalling the room and how a couple of chairs had been

pushed against the wall, Brian realized that must have been for Monty's convenience. "Okay. I'll clear the table and move our teas in there." With a smile and nod, he told him, "See you in a few."

"You don't have to do that," Monty countered, concern creasing his brow. "I can do it later." His cheeks took on a pinkish hue as he shifted in his chair. "I, uh, just really need to pee."

"Don't worry about it," Brian countered, shooing with one hand. "Do what you need to do. I don't mind." Pointing at the sink with the other, he added, "I plan to wash up there. I love pizza and wings, but it sure ends up greasy and messy."

Monty seemed to finally accept that. He turned away and headed out of the room.

Brian couldn't help but watch him go, admiring the play of muscles in the lean man's arms as he pushed his wheels. Once Monty was out of sight, he shook his head and started moving. No matter how much he responded to the man, Brian just couldn't make that leap.

Not again.

Still, Brian knew he would enjoy the view for as long as the man was around.

After washing his hands, Brian looked around the kitchen and laundry room, locating the garbage. He threw away the boxes, plates, and napkins. Then he placed the leftovers in Monty's fridge. Finally, he grabbed a cloth and wiped down the table.

Grabbing the nearly empty two-liter, Brian tucked it under his arm. He picked up a glass in each hand and made his way to the indicated study. After placing the items on a side table, Brian picked up a remote and settled in a recliner.

Brian hit a button, bringing the screen to life. As he began flipping through channels, looking at what was offered, he wondered what Monty's preferences would be.

Guess I'll have to wait until he gets back to ask him.

Even though Brian knew nothing could come of it other than friendship, he did look forward to spending time with the man.

A new friend is better than nothin'.

CHAPTER ELEVEN

"How's that feel, Monty?" Doctor Aimes asked. The man had taken over Monty's care when Doctor Lorrenz had transferred the records to the Oregon hospital. "Feel any pain?"

Monty wouldn't have minded Morgan or Donna taking over his care. Unfortunately, because they were friends, it hadn't been recommended.

Professionalism and all that.

Slowly flexing his fingers, Monty tightened his hand into a fist, then released it. "No, no pain," he told the doctor. "A little stiff and a bit of muscle soreness, but no actual pain."

"Good. I'm glad to hear it," Doctor Aimes replied with a small smile and a nod. "Remember, having the cast off does not give you leave to do any heavy lifting, handstands, or other acrobatics." While his tone sounded teasing, there was a seriousness in the doctor's eyes that told Monty that he wasn't joking. "It would be all too easy to over do it and retear something. Especially since you're still compensating from only having one usable leg."

Nodding once more, Monty assured him, "I'll follow the exercise and care sheets you gave me." He had no desire to reinjure himself, and he told the doctor so.

"Good," Doctor Aimes repeated. After a glance at his chart, he turned his attention to Monty's leg. "Now, let's talk about your leg. How's the pain level?"

For the next ten minutes, Monty and the doctor discussed his leg's healing and what to expect. Monty really didn't think it was much different than what he'd heard before. He would have the cast on for another four weeks. Then the doctor would remove it, do more x-rays, and see where they were at. Monty knew there would be at least another half-leg cast required, and he truly looked forward to that.

"You're doing really well, Monty," Doctor Aimes told him. "Healing quickly. I'm impressed."

Monty grinned. "Well, this is my first real injury, so I guess my body has plenty of stored-up healing juju."

Doctor Aimes chuckled. "Right." Patting his shoulder, he told him, "Stop at the front desk and make a follow-up appointment for four weeks." As the doctor started toward the door, he stated, "I look forward to seeing your progress."

"Thanks. Bye, doc."

"Goodbye, Monty." Then Doctor Aimes headed out the door, probably off to his next patient.

Monty took a moment to flex and release his hand a few more times before placing his hands on the wheels and starting forward. He hadn't made it to the door when Morgan entered the room. His friend glanced from his face to his hand and back again, a grin widening the handsome blond's lips.

"Nice! Got the cast off, I see." Morgan crossed to him, saying, "I spotted Doc Aimes headed into another room, so I figured you were done." Easing to Monty's side, Morgan told him, "My shift is done. Should we head somewhere to celebrate you getting your first cast off? *Mario's*?"

"I'd like that, but not *Mario's*," Monty countered. "I had that on Thursday last week."

"What?" Morgan placed his hands on his hips, his lightly glossed lips curving into a slight pout. "You got *Mario's* pizza and didn't invite me?"

Monty chuckled at his friend's antics. "Brian brought it when he came to check on me."

Morgan squealed, doing a little happy shuffle as he walked

beside him. "Really? Brian?" Grinning broadly, he stated, "I knew you guys would hit it off."

"It wasn't like that," Monty told his friend, doing his best to keep his disappointment out of his voice. "He was just being friendly." Getting a little overzealous in pushing his wheel, he hissed as a bit of pain shot through his wrist. Doing his best to cover it up when he saw Morgan's concerned glance, Monty told him, "Brian heard from Ryan about my problems with my father, and he wanted to check on me."

"Huh," Morgan murmured, hurrying a few steps past him to push the *down* button on the elevator. As Monty drew closer, Morgan frowned a little as he mumbled, "It's not like Ryan to share case information."

Monty scoffed as he stopped next to Morgan. "I think Brian is a little bit of a Nosey Nellie," he admitted. Peering up at his friend, he smirked. "He admitted to eavesdropping on Ryan's conversation."

"Well, that could happen to anyone," Morgan replied.

Monty wasn't totally sure who he was trying to defend. The doors to the elevator car opened, and Monty rolled inside. As he turned his chair, he saw Morgan joining him.

"Well, Brian also admitted to snooping in my laptop before he left a couple of weeks ago." Sighing, Monty told him, "I still had information about a job advertisement for a position in Vegas. He saw it, and he said that's why he didn't return my call."

"He wouldn't return your call just because of that?" Morgan sounded offended on his behalf. "Well, that's rude."

"In my message, I may have hinted that I'd like an at-home date and a repeat of, um . . ." Monty let his words trail off as he felt a wash of embarrassed heat fill his neck and try to creep up to his cheeks.

Morgan gasped, his blue eyes widening. "I knew it," he crowed. "Something *did* happen."

The doors of the elevator opened, saving Monty from having to answer. After all, there were several people waiting to get on, and he had no desire to talk about Brian in a crowded hospital. Monty figured he couldn't put it off forever, but he sure would try.

"So, let's go to *Applebee's*," Monty offered. "I could totally go for one of their chicken fajita rollups."

Monty felt his mouth water just at the prospect.

Morgan hummed. "I'm totally down with that," he replied with a wide smile. "Wanna split some spinach artichoke dip?"

"Oh, hell yeah." Monty grinned, anticipation filling him as he rolled through the lobby. "Hey, I thought Donna was going to take me home, but I don't see her." Pausing, Monty began pulling out his phone. "I totally forgot to call her to let her know I'm done."

"Don't worry about it." Morgan stepped behind Monty and began pushing his wheelchair. "I told her I'd get you when I realized my shift ended about the time of your appointment." As he continued pushing Monty out of the hospital, Morgan asked, "You could text her about meeting us at *Applebee's*, though. Jenna and Naomi, too."

"Jenna has a showing this afternoon, so I don't think she'll be able to come," Monty told him even as he shot off a text to all three of them. "And Naomi is working, too. Her shift ends in about an hour and a half, though, so maybe she'll be game to swing by afterward."

"Cool."

As they closed in on Morgan's sedan, Monty teased, "Where's your sexier half?"

Morgan smacked the top of Morgan's head lightly. "Keep your eyes to yourself." As Monty laughed, he heard Morgan chuckle too as he told him, "If his shift ends on time in about half an hour, he'll join us. I'll shoot him a text before I start the car." With a laugh, Morgan admitted, "He's a real stickler for that kind of stuff, being a detective and all. No texting and driving."

"Well, it *is* technically against the law," Monty teased.

"Yeah, I know," Morgan replied, smiling as he opened the door for Monty and helped him into the passenger seat. "So it's a good thing he bought me one of those awesome hands-free doohickies for Christmas. It syncs my phone with my car radio, and I can hear calls through the dash. It's super cool."

"Sweet."

Monty had heard of them, but he'd never bought one or tried to figure it out. As he adjusted his leg into a more comfortable position, he watched Morgan make his way around the hood of the car. His friend had his attention fixed on his phone in front of him, and Monty snickered, knowing he was contacting his partner.

Monty had just finished buckling his belt when Morgan slid behind the wheel. A smile was on his friend's face as he placed his phone in the cupholder. "Ryan'll meet us there."

"Good for you," Monty replied for lack of anything else to say. He definitely didn't want to admit to feeling a niggle of jealousy. His friend was so damn happy to have a partner. Until getting injured and meeting Brian, Monty had never really thought about it before.

Maybe this injury is causing a weird midlife crisis. Brian was right not to try something with me. I suddenly don't know what the hell I want out of life.

The whole situation was definitely causing him to do some soul-searching.

Monty's phone chimed, drawing him out of his thoughts — thank goodness. Opening the screen, he saw a text from Naomi. "Huh. Naomi says she'll catch us next time. She has a date."

Frowning, Monty quickly typed a response. *You better give us the guy's name, location, time info, etc. Better safe.*

"Oh, right," Morgan mused, his voice sounding a little vacant. "I wonder if it's the *UPS* guy she has the hots for."

"Hot *UPS* guy?" Monty asked absently as he read Naomi's response.

I sent all that to Jenna, but I'll forward it to you, too. I finally put on my big girl panties and asked out the UPS *guy that I've been drooling over for months. Have Morgan tell you about him. Wish me luck!*

"Yeah. He's the regular delivery guy for the boutique where she works," Morgan told him. "He took over for an older guy when he retired, I think she said."

Good luck!

After shooting off that text, Monty saw another text had come in, this one from Donna. "It looks like Donna's bringing Mitch."

"Cool." Morgan grinned as he glanced Monty's way. "There's a betting pool going on as to how long it'll be before Mitch proposes."

"They've been together as long as you and Ryan, right?"

Morgan nodded. "Just a little over. Yeah."

Giving Morgan a sly look, Monty asked, "What about you? When are you going to propose to Ryan?"

To Monty's shock, Morgan's face took on a pinkish hue as his friend whispered, "I bought a ring."

"Oh my god!" It was Monty's turn to squeal. "Really? Can I see it?"

Morgan grinned even as he shook his head. "Sure, but I don't have it on me."

"Ugh." Monty crossed his arms over his chest. "How can you be ready to propose at the *perfect moment* if you don't keep the ring on you at all times?"

With a shrug, Morgan admitted, "I don't take it to work with me. What if someone broke into the locker room and stole it?" Grimacing, he admitted, "I'd be heartbroken . . . and pissed."

"Yeah, I get it." Monty grinned at his friend. "I'm so excited for you. You know Ryan totally adores you, and you could ask while he's taking a shit on the crapper and he'd say yes."

Morgan gaped at him.

"Hey, eyes on the road," Monty barked.

Snapping his attention back to the road, Morgan corrected his lane. "That is truly the most unromantic thing I've ever heard come out of your mouth." He frowned as he glanced his way before shaking his head. "I can't believe you said that."

Shrugging, Monty muttered, "Well, it's true."

"Soooo," Morgan responded with a roll of his eyes. "I so will never do that."

"But you know Ryan would say yes."

Morgan snorted. "Of course he would. So not the point." He slowed the car, readying for the turn into the parking lot. "You've never really talked about it, but did you not have a boyfriend do something romantic for you?"

"Never had a boyfriend except that one time in college. You know that," Monty reminded his friend. "You know I wouldn't hide something like that from you."

"Yeah, I figured," Morgan answered, parking the car. Turning to face him, he asked, "Do you want one now?"

Monty blew out a quiet breath, meeting Morgan's blue-eyed gaze. "I don't know where my life is going to be in six months, Morgan." With a shrug, he admitted something that Brian had been completely right about. "It wouldn't be fair to try to start something with anyone until I have my shit figured out." Then Monty frowned and admitted, "Plus, I'd never want to put someone I care about in my father's crosshairs. It's bad enough that he's talking about coming after my friends."

"My Ryan will get that sorted," Morgan stated with conviction. "Don't you worry about that." Opening his door, he ordered, "Just sit tight. I'll be right there."

Monty moved slowly, using both hands to lift his casted leg out of the car. After swinging his good leg out, he scooted to the edge of the seat. He'd just gotten into position when Morgan arrived with his chair.

"Okay." Morgan wrapped his arm around Monty's shoulders. "On two . . . and up we go."

Snickering, Monty rocked forward with Morgan's urging, turned, and planted his butt in the chair. "What happened to two?"

Morgan grinned. "Two."

Monty laughed at Morgan's antics as he watched his buddy lock his car. When Morgan moved behind the handles, he didn't comment. While Monty could have insisted on wheeling himself, he was taking the doctor's warning to heart and not putting undue strain on his newly-mended wrist.

Plus, Monty wasn't totally confident he could get up the cement ramp.

The hostess must have spotted them coming, for she was there holding the door open when they reached it. She greeted them, and they offered their thanks. Once inside the foyer, she moved back to her station.

"Just the two of you today?" she asked, picking up menus.

"Uh, no," Morgan replied. Meeting Monty's gaze, he murmured, "I think there should be five . . . maybe six if Jenna shows? Did you hear from her?"

"Not yet," Monty replied, checking his phone once more before shaking his head.

"That's no problem," the hostess replied, picking up several more menus. "I'll put a couple of tables together so there'll be room, just in case."

"Thanks," Morgan replied.

"Right this way."

Morgan pushed Monty forward, following the woman. She

set the menus on a four-person table, then quickly moved to a second one. As soon as a waiter noticed her rearranging furniture, he quickly came to help.

Within a few minutes, two tables had been pushed together. She pulled a chair away from the head position. "Is this okay for you, sir?"

Monty hesitated. "Uh, other end, if that's okay?" He could feel his bladder telling him it was time to use the facilities. "That way, it'll be easier when I return from the men's room."

The hostess smiled. "Of course," she replied, quickly doing his bidding. Once done, she returned and told him, "Your server will be Adam." She indicated the man who'd helped her set things up. "And he's right here."

With a laugh, the hostess headed away.

"Hi, I'm Adam," the server said with a smile. "It looks like we're waiting on a few others. Can I start you off with anything until they get here?"

"I'll take an unsweetened iced tea with lemon," Monty told him.

"You go ahead, Monty," Morgan stated with a pat to his arm. "I'll order the appetizers."

"Thanks."

Monty quickly took his friend up on the offer and headed into the bathroom. Fortunately, the handicapped stall was spacious, allowing him plenty of room to maneuver. He did his business, returned to his chair, and headed out to wash his hands.

While Monty didn't think he'd taken all that long, by the time he returned to the table everyone had arrived. Except, instead of Jenna sitting in the seat to the left of his empty space, there was someone else. Monty felt his breath catch in his chest upon spotting the handsome Native American.

Damn. Brian looks so hot in jeans and a pull-over with his wet hair slicked back from those sexy-as-hell cheekbones.

Except, what the hell is he doing here?

Chapter Twelve

B rian wasn't entirely certain how Ryan had talked him into coming. The detective had spotted him leaving the gym, having worked out for an hour after his shift had ended. The friendly man had grinned while beckoning.

"Hey, man," Ryan had greeted. "You headed home for dinner?"

"I am," Brian had confirmed, eyeing the man curiously.

"I'm meeting Morgan at *Applebee's* with a few others," Ryan had told him, clapping him on the shoulder while grinning broadly. "Join us."

Brian had only hesitated a second before he'd conceded. "Okay."

In truth, Brian had thought the few others would be Ryan's detective partner on the force, Carl, as well as Carl's partner, Vincent. Maybe their good buddies, Trace and Laramie, too.

I sure as hell never thought it would be Morgan's crowd . . . and Monty.

Damn, he looks good. No cast on his arm anymore. Playtime would be so much fun now that he has both hands.

Brian did his best to push those thoughts out of his mind. "Hey, Monty," he greeted as the handsome man rolled up to the empty position on his right. It truly hadn't occurred to him that that was the reason there wasn't a chair there. "Morgan tells me you're celebrating getting your cast off your wrist. Congrats."

"Thanks, Brian," Monty responded with a grin. Lifting his

right hand, he made a fist, then released it to wiggle his fingers. "It's so nice to get a little bit of mobility back. I'll be fitted for crutches in another week," Monty told him, clearly pleased. "They want just a little more time to build up strength."

"I'm happy for you," Brian replied honestly, appreciating the happiness clearly written all over the cute blond's face. "You'll be back on your feet soon."

"Yep." Leaning close, Monty lowered his voice as he winked conspiratorially, "I have a swing out back that I can't wait to enjoy."

Brian chuckled, even as Morgan—who was sitting across from him and to Monty's right—whipped his attention to Monty and snapped, "Hey. No swinging while you're healing." His eyes narrowed as he threatened, "Don't make me find it and take it down."

Monty straightened as he laughed. "I meant a regular old wooden swing." His eyes twinkled with mirth. "You know. It's in a tree. You park your butt on it and relax a little."

Morgan stared at him with narrowed eyes, as if gauging his friend's truthfulness. "That better be all it is."

Lifting his hand, three fingers up and the others tucked in, Monty told him, "Scout's honor."

Scoffing, Morgan shook his head. "You were never a scout."

Monty shrugged. "How do you know? I could have been." With an innocent smile, Monty added, "We did meet in college, after all."

A second later, a bit of tortilla chip came sailing toward Monty, hitting him in the chest.

"Hey," Monty cried, focusing down the table. "What was that for?"

Donna smirked at him, completely unrepentant. "*I* knew you growing up," she claimed. "And you *so* were never a scout."

Monty grinned broadly as he picked up the chip off his lap. "Nope, I wasn't." Reaching forward, he scooped up a dollop of the artichoke dip that was on Morgan's plate, ignoring his friend's indignant cry as he waggled his brows. Before plopping the chip into his mouth, Monty stated, "Had ya goin' though, didn't I?"

Morgan snickered even as he rolled his eyes. "No way."

Brian could see, just from the way Monty laughed, that he didn't believe his friend. The pretty man's hazel eyes were sparkling, drawing him in. Brian felt his heart pound in his chest as heat sizzled within his veins, swiftly flowing south.

"Here's your iced tea, sir," the waiter stated, setting the drink before him. Straightening, he looked around at those occupying the table. "Is everyone ready to order?"

Focusing on his iced tea, Brian picked it up even as he glanced around at the others.

"Yep," Monty replied, smiling at Adam. "I'll take the chicken fajita rollup, please. Can I get the mashed potatoes instead of fries?"

"Sure can," Adam confirmed, jotting it down on the tablet he was carrying. He turned his attention to Brian. "And for you, sir?"

Considering Brian had been too distracted by spotting Monty rolling toward the table to finish looking at the menu, he went with something that was always good. "Your bacon cheeseburger, please." After a second of hesitation, he added, "And a side salad instead of the fries."

Adam nodded. "I can do that." Then he moved on. After having finished everyone's orders, Adam glanced around the table again. "Is everything on one check?"

The man at the other end of the table, who'd been introduced as Mitch, indicated himself and Donna. "We're together."

Ryan, who sat kitty-corner to Brian, indicated himself, Morgan, and Monty. "I'll cover the three of us."

Brian wasn't certain what came over him, but he shook his head. "No, you don't," he countered. He pointed at Monty. "Put his on my ticket."

"Oooo, I'm being fought over. It's like tug-o-war," Monty teased as he glanced between them. Grinning up at Adam, he stated, "But actually, put everything on *my* ticket. I'm celebrating, so it should be my treat."

"That's right, we're celebrating you getting your arm cast off," Donna countered from where she sat to Brian's left. "That means you *don't* pay, silly." Then she waggled her brows and said, "You can put him on mine and Mitch's tab."

Adam lifted his hands as he laughed. "How about I put the man of the hour on his own separate ticket, and you all can fight amongst yourselves." Before anyone could respond, Adam quickly scurried away.

Smart man.

Brian relaxed in his seat as he watched Morgan and Donna begin to softly argue about who was going to pay. Considering they were both doctors, he figured it really was foolish for him to jump in, and if he was honest with himself, he wasn't entirely certain why he had. For some reason, hearing Ryan state that he was going to pay for Monty had struck a chord with him.

So odd.

It almost felt as if Ryan were trying to . . . show him up, perhaps—show him up in front of a guy he was trying to impress.

Even thinking it seemed odd to Brian. After all, Ryan had never been competition to him. Until Carl had come out as dating a firefighter nearly a decade before, they hadn't run in even close to the same circles. Brian had been just a couple of years out of the academy, and Ryan had been a detective.

"Hey. Brian."

Hearing Monty's quiet voice calling his name, Brian pulled his attention away from the cubes in his iced tea glass. They really weren't *that* interesting. He knew he'd just been zoning out.

It'd been a long day.

"Yeah?" Brian smiled at Monty.

"It was awful nice of you to offer to pay for me." Monty peered at him with an almost shy expression on his face. "Thank you."

Brian roved his gaze over Monty's handsome features. Unable to help himself, he leaned forward and teased, "Does that mean you're going to let me be the one to claim your ticket?"

The sound of Monty's soft snickers caused Brian's heart to trip in his chest.

Damn. Why do I find that such a gorgeous sound?

Leaning toward him, Monty rested his left elbow on the arm of his wheelchair. "No," he murmured, shaking his head. Perhaps to soften his rejection, he told him, "If I were to let anyone claim my ticket, it'd be Morgan, because this was his idea, but—" Monty paused suddenly. Straightening in his chair, he wrinkled his nose. "Eww, eww, eww. That sounded so wrong."

Brian barked a laugh, all his disappointment fading in light of Monty's crinkled nose and clear creeped-out factor.

"What?" Brian teased. Waggling his brows, he asked, "You don't want . . . Morgan . . . *claiming your ticket*?"

"Stop it. That's so wrong!" Monty hissed, shaking his head even as his cheeks pinkened. "He's like a brother to me." Monty gave an exaggerated, all-body shudder.

Still chuckling, Brian continued to grin. "You said it, and it was your mind that went into the gutter."

"Hey." Monty pointed his finger at him. "Your mind went right there with me, so you have no room to talk."

Brian couldn't help sweeping his gaze over the cute man's lean torso. "Well, you can always move over so I can float on by, because I have some other things I'd really like to dwell on." Then, realizing he was flirting—thereby sending mixed signals—Brian cleared his throat and straightened. "Sorry, Monty," he muttered, shaking his head.

Monty offered him a slight smile. "It's okay. I get it." Pointing at the artichoke dip, he asked, "Have you tried this yet? It's amazing."

Thankful that Monty was willing to let him off the hook, Brian shook his head. "No. I didn't order it." When he saw Monty's brows lift on his forehead, he explained, "I didn't want to offend whoever wanted it by stealing some without permission."

Nodding once in understanding, Monty told him, "Well, I had Morgan order it for me while I went to the men's room, so feel free to try it." As if to reinforce his words, he grabbed a couple of the small plates sitting in a stack—there were four left—near the middle of the table. "Here ya go." Monty placed one in front of himself and the other in front of Brian. "Ooo, and they ordered mozzarella sticks." Grinning, he pointed, "Can you hold that out to me so I can grab one, please?"

Brian was happy to comply. Reaching in front of Donna, he picked up the plate and held it out to Monty. After the healing man took one, Brian returned it to the table in nearly the same position.

Glancing left, Brian realized he'd drawn Donna's attention. She smiled even as she eyed him speculatively. Brian sort of felt like a bug under a microscope.

Just great.

"So, Jenna said you stopped by last Thursday and took Monty some pizza," the lady doctor began.

"Donna." Monty growled her name in clear warning. "Don't."

Donna opened her mouth, then snapped it shut again. Offering Brian a sweet smile, she shrugged. "I was just going to say that it was nice of you. Monty can use more friends." Her expression sobered. "Especially with everything going on with him."

While Brian knew beyond a shadow of a doubt that *that* hadn't been what Donna was going to say, he felt grateful for Monty's interruption. "Everyone can use more friends," he rumbled. "Or so I've heard."

"Ugh." Donna's eyes narrowed, and she curled her lip.

At first, Brian thought Donna's reaction was to his rather cliché comment.

Then Donna muttered, "Speaking of *problems*."

Brian followed where Donna was looking and spotted a tall, thickset blond man in a suit, heading in their direction. His thick hair was arranged in a wavy business style. In Brian's mind, the guy's hazel eyes seemed a little familiar, although he knew he'd never seen the man before. Plus, there was a definite coldness glittering within their depths.

"Montgomery," the man growled, stopping a couple of steps behind Monty's right shoulder. "What the hell is the meaning of those papers delivered to me?"

As the man leaned down and practically hissed the words at Monty, Brian saw the way Monty's body tensed.

Monty turned his head just a little, and Brian imagined the man was looking at him out of the corner of his eye. "Those papers were perfectly self-explanatory, Cornelian, even without the officer explaining them," he responded. Although his voice was soft, there was a definite hint of steel within it. "That means you're not to be within fifty feet of me. You're in breach."

Cornelian? This is Monty's asshat father?

Brian figured the sexy acrobat had to have gotten his build from his mother.

Cornelian sneered. "Listen here, you little—"

Ryan rose to his feet, tossing his cloth napkin to the table. "Mister Worshack, I'll give you this one warning."

Seeing the way Ryan stalked slowly behind Morgan's chair

to face off with Cornelian, Brian quickly popped up to offer his fellow boy in blue back-up. He ignored his napkin as it fell to the floor. Keeping his hands loose at his sides, Brian was pleased to see that his six-foot-one height, while not as wide as Cornelian's, gave him an inch on the man, allowing him to look down at the asshole.

"You have been served with a restraining order against this man," Ryan continued, stopping near his side. "Please return to your table and do not approach him again. Don't think we'll give you a second warning."

"This is my son," Cornelian snarled, peering disdainfully at Ryan. His eyes narrowed as he glanced toward Brian before returning to Ryan. "I can talk to him whenever and wherever I wish."

"Not according to the law, Mister Worshack," Ryan countered. "Again, return to your seat, or I'll be forced to arrest you." Ryan's deep voice hardened as he added, "And make no mistake, the next time you break the restraining order, you *will* be arrested."

Brian watched a muscle tick in Cornelian's jaw, and his face began to take on a distinctively angry shade of red. For a few seconds, he thought the man would start shit, and they would end up having to haul him in. Brian couldn't say he would mind too much.

After a snarl, Cornelian pushed past Ryan, knocking his shoulder into the shorter man as he passed him. Brian thought it was a little funny because while Ryan was just shy of six feet, putting him an inch shorter than Monty's father, the man was solid muscle . . . and he didn't move a step. Cornelian actually bounced to the side as if he were a ricocheting pinball.

Cornelian caught his balance, used his palms to rub down his suit jacket, then stalked from the restaurant.

As Brian watched, a small, slender blonde woman with pinched features scurried after him, sending a scathing look in Monty's direction.

Yep. Takes after his mom . . . in looks anyway.

Following her was a pair of men that screamed thugs, from their brutish looks to their suits with obvious bulges under their jackets.

Good grief. What's Monty's father mixed up in?

Brian exchanged a look with Ryan, knowing he wasn't the only one with such thoughts. After a chin dip of thanks to Brian, Ryan returned to his seat. He picked up his napkin and spread it over his lap. Smiling at Morgan, Ryan reached for a mozzarella stick as if nothing had happened.

Following the other man's example, Brian settled back in his seat. He grabbed his iced tea and took a healthy swallow of the cold liquid, feeling the chill sweep down his throat. The cool fluid helped soothe his frustration. Brian set his glass back down and caught Monty looking at him, so he offered the man a reassuring smile.

The small smile Brian received in response caused his heart to flutter in his chest.

So weird.

Then Monty reached over and rested his hand over the back of Brian's. "Thanks," he whispered.

Brian shrugged. "Didn't do much," he replied just as quietly.

Monty hummed as if in disagreement, but just then, Adam arrived with their food, and the moment passed.

CHAPTER THIRTEEN

"Uh, thanks again for taking me home," Monty stated, glancing at Brian as he entered his area of town. "I'm sorry Donna guilted you into this."

Brian shook his head once, slowing as they headed up the side of the hill toward his home. "I wasn't guilted into anything, Monty." Reaching over, he squeezed his upper thigh. "Donna had to take a conference call with another surgeon, and Mitch was taking her home to do it." Then Brian scoffed softly as he muttered, "And did you see the looks that Ryan and Morgan were giving each other? Yeah, they needed to get home as fast as possible."

Monty felt his cheeks heat as he recalled exactly what Brian was talking about. "They, uh, thought they were being subtle."

Snorting, Brian shook his head. "Well, they failed." With a smirk, he added, "Of course, I *am* trained to spot things, being a cop and all."

Chuckling softly, Monty nodded as he saw his home come into view. He felt a slight twist in his gut, realizing his time with Brian was about to come to an end. Nibbling his bottom lip, he thought quickly.

Before Brian could park out front, Monty asked, "Will you park around back again, please?"

The man nodded, although he didn't say anything.

Brian parked in front of the large shop that housed the caretaker's quarters over the top of it. After turning off his SUV's engine, he hit the button to pop the rear hatch and climbed out. Monty opened his door and carefully began maneuvering out, noticing Brian at the back, pulling out his wheelchair.

I can hardly wait for those crutches.

After parking the chair near the passenger door, Brian rested his hand on Monty's upper arm. He offered support as Monty slid out, while still mostly allowing Monty to do it on his own. Still, Monty could see that Brian kept a sharp eye on him, and he knew that the officer would step in if he showed any signs of falling.

Something about that kind of watchfulness, being certain he was okay yet offering a bit of independence, warmed something within Monty. On top of that, Monty had enjoyed the flashes of playful flirting Brian would slip into on occasion at the restaurant. Monty never called attention to it, even when Brian would realize what he was doing and pull back again. Monty knew the officer was just as attracted to him as Monty was to Brian, but he wouldn't do anything about it, either.

Damn. I could really get used to this kind of attention, but I know I need to be certain this is what I really want.

Monty didn't want to hurt Brian for the world, even by mistake.

After settling in the chair, Monty allowed Brian to push him up the ramp to the back deck. He opened his door, and they entered the house. Once they were in the dining room, Brian paused and focused his attention on Monty.

"Is there anything you need before I head out?" Brian asked.

Licking his lips, Monty watched Brian follow the movement with his eyes. There was definitely something Monty wanted, but he wondered if he could get Brian to give it to him. Deciding to take a chance, Monty nodded.

"What can I help with?" Brian immediately asked.

Lifting a hand, Monty beckoned. "Will you come down here, please?" he asked softly.

Brian hesitated a second before bending at the waist. "What's wrong?" Resting a hand on the arm of Monty's wheelchair, he focused a worried gaze upon him. "Are you worried about your father?"

"While I *am* worried about my father," Monty admitted, unwilling to lie to the man. After all, he'd overheard his father making demands to his underlings while living at home. "That's not what this is about."

Reaching up, Monty cradled Brian's jaw in his palms. He noticed the way the bigger man tensed, feeling it beneath his fingers. When Brian began to draw away, Monty quickly slipped his left hand behind the man's neck.

"Wait," Monty whispered. "Please."

While Monty knew Brian could easily pull away, Brian didn't, stilling in his hold, and heat and pleasure uncoiled within Monty's body.

"I know you said nothing could happen between us, but" — Monty hesitated, then pulled on his big boy undies and admitted — "I really want to see if your kiss is just as amazing as I remember." Applying a bit of pressure to the back of Brian's neck, he teased the thumb of his other hand along his jaw. "Please?"

Brian seemed to be searching his expression for several heartbeats. A muscle in his jaw ticked under Monty's palm. Then Brian licked his lips before closing the distance between them.

Monty tipped his head back a little as he leaned forward, meeting Brian's approach. He felt the other man seal his lips over his own, and he immediately opened. To Monty's pleasure, Brian took the offer, and a second later, Monty found himself with a mouthful of questing, teasing, roving tongue.

Groaning as the kiss went from zero to a hundred in two seconds flat, Monty hung on for the ride, doing his best to give as good as he got. He wrapped one arm around Brian's shoulders and gripped tightly. Monty slid the hand up Brian's jaw to sink his fingers into the man's thick, black hair. The strands were just as soft as he imagined, and he moaned into the other man's mouth.

Brian responded with a growl of his own as he tore his lips from Monty's. His chest heaved as his full lips gleamed in the soft light coming from the bar pendant lighting. Swallowing hard, Brian stared down at him, his black eyes seeming to glitter with some intense emotion.

"Wow," Monty whispered, uncaring how breathless he sounded. "Th-That . . . yeah."

"Yeah," Brian responded huskily, even as he eased from Monty's hold. For a second, he remained partially bent over Monty. Then he sighed. "Have a good night, Monty," he whispered. Ducking his head, Brian pecked a kiss to Monty's temple before easing away and heading toward the door. "Don't forget to throw the deadbolt after I leave." Reaching the door, Brian half-turned and peered at Monty over his shoulder, and he offered him a warm smile. "If you need me, call me."

Then Brian disappeared into the mud room. The soft click of the door heralded his exit.

Blowing out a breath, Monty let out a deep sigh. He rubbed at his cheeks, feeling the heat on them. Arousal simmered through his body, and he reached down to adjust his hard dick.

As much as it sucked, Monty understood why Brian had walked away. With a sigh, he moved his hands to his wheels and headed to the back door. Doing as Brian had encouraged, Monty deadbolted the door. After that, he checked the rest of the house, making certain everything was locked up tight.

Monty headed to his room and went through his evening routine. Lying in bed, he draped a hand towel over his waist.

He slid his hands underneath it.

With one hand, Monty gripped his still-hard length in his right palm. He cupped his balls lightly with his left. As he began jacking his long, slender length, Monty sighed deeply at finally having his dominant hand free of the cast. Jacking off with his left just hadn't been the same.

Tipping his head back, Monty relaxed into his hold. He drew up images of Brian's strong features and intense dark eyes. His full lips, gleaming with the moisture of their kiss, caused Monty's heart to speed up in his chest. When Monty recalled the way his chest heaved and his breathing came in ragged breaths, he moaned roughly as a shudder went through him.

When Monty imaged the soft feel of Brian's thick black hair running through his fingers, and maybe being wrapped around his heated cock, Monty felt his balls begin to tighten. He sped up his tugs as he rolled his balls across his palm. With his pinky finger, Monty reached back and teased the sensitive skin behind them.

Monty rubbed his thumb over his crown on the next up-stroke, gathering the pre-cum there. Swiping it down his length, he imagined the tunnel of his hand was the tight heat of Brian's mouth. The dampness of his pre-cum was Brian's saliva.

The tingle at the base of Monty's spine intensified. Squeezing his balls, he sped up his strokes even more. His breathing came in ragged pants, and the sweet zings of his impending orgasm caused his gut to flutter.

A second later, Monty was there, his body tumbling over the edge into sweet oblivion. His seed burst from his prick in sharp, bliss-inducing bursts. He groaned Brian's name on ragged gasps as his senses soared in sweet ecstasy.

Drifting on his endorphins, Monty still wondered what it would be like to feel that for real. He knew Brian's hand felt amazing. Monty guessed the man's mouth would feel ten-times as fantastic.

Monty sighed deeply, lethargy coming over him. He used the hand towel to wipe away the seed it hadn't caught before tossing it over the side of his bed. With a grunt, Monty relaxed into his pillow and allowed his mind to drift on the dredges of his release's endorphins.

It didn't take long to slip into sleep, and if he was mentally wishing that Brian was there to hold him, only he would know.

The following morning, Monty was sitting at the dining room table drinking a cup of coffee and eating a couple of pieces of buttered toast when Donna arrived. He wasn't totally with it, still waiting for his *ibuprofen* to kick in. Monty realized he'd strained his leg a little while jacking off the previous evening, not that he would ever admit that to anyone.

"Hey, Monty!" Donna called after Monty heard the front door open. "It's me."

"I'm in the dining room," Monty hollered back.

Monty placed his cell phone back on the table. When the locks had clicked, he'd grabbed it, and instinct had him pulling up Brian's number. The screen was still lit when Donna walked in, and her gaze fell on the device.

"Oh, already texting Brian first thing," Donna teased, winking lasciviously. "Or are you sexting?" Her tone turned suggestive as she asked, "Did you have a fantastic evening?"

Monty eyed his friend over the brim of his coffee mug. "I had a good evening," he conceded. "Thanks for meeting me for an impromptu dinner." Humming as he thought back on getting together with his friends, Monty murmured, "You know, I realize now that I really missed you guys." Cocking his head, he admitted, "My life really was all work and very little play."

111

"Aaaand, how was the *play* last night?" Donna placed her purse on the counter as she crossed to the coffee pot to pour her own cup of joe. "Have a good time?"

Scoffing, Monty decided to share, "Well, Brian gave me a goodnight kiss, then went home."

Pouring a dash of cream into her coffee, Donna frowned at him in disappointment. "That's it?" She crossed to the table and settled on a chair one down from him. "But—" Her confusion was clear. "You all have chemistry. I thought"—she shrugged—"you know, you'd have a different kind of cast removal celebration once you got home."

Monty didn't really want to get into the reasons why Brian was putting the brakes on anything between them. "Sorry to disappoint you," he replied instead. With a scoff, he stated, "I mean, come on. I'm hardly in a position to start anything. Plus, I don't know where I'm going to be in six months."

Donna narrowed her eyes as she took a sip of her coffee. "Maybe you need to think about that then." Setting her cup on the table, she reached across the space between them and gripped Monty's hand. With a smile, Donna told him, "We've missed having you around."

Flipping his hand, Monty admitted, "I've really missed being here." He peered into Donna's sympathetic blue eyes and told her, "I didn't realize just how much."

Monty returned his hand to his mug and lifted it to his lips. "You know." Resting his elbows on the table, he stared at her over the brim. "Naomi mentioned the idea of opening some kind of gym." Frowning, Monty asked, "Do you think I could actually do that?"

Humming, Donna seemed to give that the thought it deserved. She took a sip of her coffee. Then she leaned back in her chair, lifting her legs to sit cross-legged on it.

"I really think that all depends on you," Donna mused, tipping her head a little in thought. "I really never thought of you as a manager, but if you had a good one of those, I bet you would make a fantastic teacher of . . . well . . . certain types of classes."

Nodding slowly, Monty thought about that. "I did always love it when our circus had an open house day."

Monty recalled the kids who'd loved climbing the ladder to the hanging rings. Their squeals of pleasure when they grabbed them and rode them to the safety net before letting go to tumble upon it had always brought a smile to his face. Then there were others who loved walking on the tight-rope . . . with a little helping hand. Even helping the odd adult who wanted to try things had been a hoot.

"You just had a thought," Donna stated knowingly.

Nodding, Monty admitted, "Naomi said something about a ninja warrior gym, and I looked it up. There are a lot of gym-nastic aspects to that, and some of the obstacles they have to do are absolutely fascinating." In truth, Monty was itching to give some of them a try. "I wonder if something like that might be a good fit."

"Is there one around here?" Donna asked curiously.

Monty shook his head before sipping his coffee.

To Monty's surprise, Donna grinned widely. "You've al-ready looked into it."

Feeling his cheeks heat, Monty admitted, "I've already looked into places that are for rent, but the idea of figuring out renovations is really . . . overwhelming." When he'd started looking at construction prices, his brain had started shutting down.

"That's what friends are for," Donna told him.

"Huh?" Frowning, Monty told her, "What friends? I don't have any friends in construction."

Donna grinned broadly. "*You* may not, but I know people that do."

"You do?"

"Yup." Donna giggled. "Friends of friends. That sort of thing." When Monty remained silent, processing that, Donna sighed, smiling at him in understanding. "You've been going at it alone way too long, Monty. Let us help you."

"You *are* helping me," Monty countered, confused. He waved toward his casted leg. "I wouldn't have gotten by without you all," he said, referring to Donna and their group of friends.

"Then let us continue helping you," Donna encouraged, her expression lighting up. "Did you know Ryan and Carl helped their friend with a barn-raising a number of years back?"

"Seriously?" Monty hadn't heard about that.

"Yep," Donna confirmed with a sharp nod. "I think if they can do that, they'll know people who can help you build a gym." Then she laughed as she added, "Once you decide what kind you want anyway."

"Huh."

Monty stared vacantly across the room as ideas poured through his mind.

CHAPTER FOURTEEN

Standing at the sink in his precinct's breakroom, Brian focused on the coffee mug he was washing. He quickly scrubbed it down before rinsing it. Placing it in the drain board, he rinsed the cloth, rung it out, then draped it over the metal basket's side.

Brian plucked a paper towel from the roll and dried his hands before using the same towel to wipe most of the dampness from his mug. After tossing the wet cloth, he turned toward the coffee maker. He'd been annoyed to find the carafe empty and had restarted it before washing his mug.

Why can't whoever takes the last of the coffee do the polite thing and restart a fresh pot?

Nearly finished.

Setting his mug near the pot, Brian headed to the refrigerator. As he pulled out his sack lunch, he knew why he was so annoyed. Brian had finally found someone who was sexy as sin and wanted him back . . . and he couldn't let himself go after him. He'd gone back and forth with the idea of just trying to have a good time with Monty.

Except, Brian knew, if he did that, he would fall hard and fast. He knew he'd always been that way. It was why one-night stands were so difficult for him. Brian was a possessive bastard in regards to a lover, and he knew it.

Brian placed his reusable plastic sack on the table just as he heard the coffee pot gurgling, heralding the completion of the coffee cycle. Returning to the counter, he watched as the last couple of drips plopped into the glass carafe.

Maybe I really should just enjoy what Monty's offering. He never promised forever. If I kept that front and center in my mind, maybe I could do a fling with him.

Hell, it's better than my right hand.

After sharing that kiss with Monty a week and a half before, Brian had jacked off to memories of the sexy acrobat every evening . . . and sometimes in the shower. He'd recalled the way he'd tasted, the way his tongue had felt sensually sliding against his own, and the feel of his erection filling his palm when he'd jacked him off. Brian had imagined the feel of Monty's pretty pink lips wrapped around his erection as he sucked him like a hoover.

Predictably, Brian's dick began to swell at his thoughts.

Gritting his teeth, Brian picked up the carafe and filled his mug. He really did need to get laid. Except, he'd even gone out to a club over the weekend, but he hadn't been able to find one damn man he was interested in allowing near his dick.

It had been a frustrating — and depressing — evening, as well as another evening with his right hand.

Good grief. This has got to stop.

Isn't he worth trying for? Give him a reason to stick around?

As Brian returned to the table with his coffee, he decided he needed to see the man again. He needed to talk to him. If there was even a chance at having something with Monty, Brian knew he should take the risk, no matter how difficult or scary it might seem.

Wouldn't Monty be worth it?

Brian had just settled at the table when he heard the door to the break room swing open. He looked that way, surprise filling him when he saw detectives Ryan and Carl enter.

Huh. What are they doing down here?

"Hey, Brian," Ryan greeted, heading his way. "Tiny told us you were on break," he told him, referring to a fairly new beat cop who was, in fact, huge. "Hope you don't mind us interrupting your lunch."

"Not at all, guys." Brian used a foot to push out a nearby chair. "Take a load off."

In truth, Brian wouldn't mind company. It would keep him from getting too sucked into his thoughts.

"What can I help you with?" Brian asked. While they were taking a seat, he pulled out his food — an already peeled orange, a cup of cheese cubes mixed with peanuts, and a container of chicken Caesar salad. Glancing their way as he peeled the lid off, Brian took in their serious expressions. "Uh, what's wrong?"

"We know you've started to get close to Monty," Carl started without preamble. He rested his forearms on the table, leaning forward. "We wanted your take on whether this news would be better coming from us or you."

Well, shit. That doesn't sound ominous or anything. What the hell's going on with the pretty acrobat?

Hey, wait a second.

"Uh, Monty and I are friends. Well, getting there, anyway," Brian hedged slowly. "I'm not certain why something would be better coming from me."

Carl grimaced as he turned his attention to Ryan. "I see what you mean."

Ryan shrugged. "You remember how long it took me to get over my ex," he muttered, scrubbing his hand over his beard. "Years. Years and years."

Scoffing, Carl nodded. "We both know you're interested in more," he stated, returning his focus to Brian. "But it looks like you're holding back because of your asshat ex." Dipping his chin in a nod, Carl stated, "I get it. I really do." Then his brows furrowed as Carl pinned him with a serious gaze. "But don't let a great thing pass you by because you're scared."

"What?" Brian glanced between the pair, trying to figure out what the hell was going on.

Are these two playing matchmaker?

Instead of answering, Carl's eyes widened as he snapped

his attention back to Ryan. "If Monty does decide to open a gym, he's going to need to make certain this guy or some dude sympathetic to him doesn't infiltrate his staff."

Even more confusion flooded Brian. "What the hell are you guys talking about?" Latching onto a few of the words Carl had uttered, he asked, "Monty's considering opening a gym?"

If he did that, would that mean he would need to stay in the area?

Brian felt a surge of hope that immediately caused butterflies to flutter within his belly. In the next second, he felt guilt.

Could it be true? Would he really do that?

God damn it. I can't let him take all the risk. I'm such a pussy!

Even just a few months with the wonderful man would be worth its weight in gold. I seriously need to make it up to him.

Then Brian wondered about all the other things Carl was spouting but totally not explaining. "Hey," he growled, rapping his knuckles on the *Formica* tabletop to get their attention. "What the hell are you guys talking about?" When neither one of them said a word, just continuing to stare at him, Brian snapped, "Tell me what the fuck is going on."

After Carl and Ryan exchanged a glance, the pair began explaining. With every word they spoke, every fact they shared, Brian felt his breath tripping in his chest for an all new reason.

Someone had it in for Monty, and there were no prizes for guessing who.

Pulling up to Monty's house that evening, Brian hesitated, wondering if he should knock on the front door or go around back. He figured he'd better stick to the front. Parking, Brian shut off his SUV and hurried up the front walk to the porch.

Brian rung the bell and waited . . . and waited. Frowning, he rung the bell a second time. While he could hear the sound reverberating through the interior, as soon as it faded, there was nothing.

Frustration and worry filling him, Brian tried the knob. He felt a measure of trepidation as well as relief to find the door locked.

Okay. Now what.

Leaving his SUV parked out front, Brian stepped off the porch and began striding around the side of the house. He hurried down the side path to the rear. Once he reached the back deck, Brian took the steps two at a time.

Brian had just lifted his hand to knock on the back door when he heard a voice call, "Excuse me, young man. Do you need somethin'?"

Pivoting, Brian spotted an older gentleman standing at the second-story landing leading to the apartment over the large shop. The caretaker. He took a couple of steps in the man's direction.

"I'm Brian O'Reilly," he declared. "Monty's friend. I thought he'd be home and was looking for him."'

"A friend of Monty's, ya say?" The man squinted down at him. "Can't say's I recognize ya. If'n I call Miss Donna or Miss Jenna, what will they say?"

"They know me," Brian claimed. "They'll tell you." He mentally crossed his fingers that Jenna would indeed confirm that he was a friend. "Just tell them that Officer Brian O'Reilly is looking for Monty." Then something else occurred to him. "Or I can call Morgan. Maybe he'll know if Monty ended up heading somewhere this evening."

"Officer, eh?"

The man certainly didn't sound too trusting. Part of Brian appreciated that Monty had someone so protective looking out for him. Another part, however, was getting tired of being delayed.

"Yes, sir." Still, Brian continued to force himself to be polite. Biting his tongue, he refused to extrapolate.

Brian heard the man hum as he squinted at his phone. He barely resisted rolling his eyes. Instead, he rested his hip against the railing and waited.

Besides, if I end up starting something with Monty, I better get on the good side of this man.

After a few seconds, Brian saw the man bring the phone to his ear. "Yes, sir. Sorry to bother you, sir. There's an Officer Brian O'Reilly here lookin' fer ya." The man snapped his mouth shut, and Brian was just close enough to see his gray eyebrows shoot up his forehead. "Yes, sir. I'll tell him, sir." After another heartbeat, the caretaker added, "Thank you, sir. Same to you. Have a nice evening."

Then the man returned his focus to Brian. "Head through that there trellis." He pointed to a trellis separating the rose garden from some nicely sculpted hedges. "Take the left fork. You'll see him after a minute."

"Thank you, sir," Brian stated, taking the steps back down two at a time. He hurried past the rose beds, noticing a couple of the beds had a few weeds in them. "Maybe another time."

The caretaker appears old, after all.

Brian took the trail through the trellis, and the trees quickly closed in overhead. He immediately spotted the branch in the trail and headed left, even as he wondered how Monty had made it through there. After fifty paces, the trail bent to the right . . . and opened up into a small, gorgeous clearing.

Unable to help it, Brian had to pause to take it all in. The space couldn't have been more than fifty feet wide by thirty feet deep. There were trees lining left and right—not exceptionally tall, but enough to block out the neighboring homes. On the far side—which was slightly sloped downward— Brian spotted a black, wrought-iron fence. Beyond that was . . . a view of the valley. Trees, homes, roads, and more stretched as far as the eye can see.

So this is the million-dollar view that people pay for.

Brian had no trouble dismissing it.

Instead, Brian found his attention snagged by the man sitting on an old, wood-plank swing off to the left. The old oak must have been there for a century, and the ropes were tied high within the foliage. They must have been secured through a couple of holes, for a bit of rope dangled beneath the plank on either end, barely drawing Brian's attention as it swayed.

The movement was caused by a good leg planted on the ground, the calf flexing and releasing, making the occupant sway — Monty. Brian noticed the crutches lying on the ground to the man's left, telling him how he'd gotten out there.

Unable to stay away, Brian stalked across the small clearing. He saw the way Monty's head tilted just a smidge in his direction, giving him a view of the man's handsome features. Brian admired his toned frame, even half-hidden by the hoodie he wore — *because I know better* — and recalled how good it had felt pressed against him, under his fingertips.

Without saying a word, Brian eased up behind Monty. He rested his hands on the man's shoulders, pleased that he didn't feel any tension there. Sliding them down his back to his sides, he hunched a little. Finally, Brian slipped his arms around Monty's waist as he lowered himself to one knee behind him.

As Brian rubbed over Monty's torso, tracing over the oh-so-nicely delineated lines of his chest, he rested his chin on Monty's shoulder. "Hey, Monty," he murmured, enjoying the feel of the other man's firm flesh — even covered in fabric — beneath his own. "Thanks for letting your caretaker tell me where you are."

Monty nodded nearly imperceptibly. "Hey, Brian." Turning his head a little farther, he muttered, "Figured it'd be important for you to stop by."

Damn. Guess I had that coming.

Brian scoffed, turning his head a bit so he pressed his forehead into Monty's shoulder. "A few things, I suppose. Good and bad." Lifting his head, Brian met Monty's gaze squarely, knowing he had to be totally honest with the guy. "I hope, anyway."

"Good and bad?" Monty's slender brows furrowed. "How so?"

Inhaling deeply, Brian bit the bullet and declared, "Ryan and Carl found proof that your father's trying to discreetly orchestrate your death."

Monty immediately gaped, a gasp escaping him. "I sure as hell hope that's the bad thing."

After swallowing hard, Brian whispered, "Only you can tell me." Holding the sexy man's gaze, he whispered, "I'm so sorry I've been such a coward. Will you, uh . . ." Brian cleared his throat once before growling, "Well, I want to try with you. Will you try with me?"

For several long seconds, Monty stared at him. The shock registered in his hazel eyes first before his jaw sagged open. When he shook his head once, Brian feared the man was denying him.

Except, then Monty barked, "*Now?* You ask me that *now?* After you tell me my father's trying to kill me?"

Brian thought about that for a few seconds, then winced. Grimacing, he smiled at Monty.

"Bad timing?"

CHAPTER FIFTEEN

Monty thought about that for a few seconds. Was it bad timing? Sort of, but then he admitted just how much he was enjoying Brian's strong arms wrapped around his waist as well as the way he'd been nuzzling his neck. He wanted more of that . . . more of everything.

With a sigh, Monty told him, "It's never a bad time if it's with you." Even as Brian grinned at him, he winced. "Wow," Monty muttered. "That sounded really cheesy."

"Cheesy or not, I liked it," Brian told him, pressing a kiss to the side of his neck. "Very much."

Tipping his head to the side, Monty offered more room, and Brian took advantage, placing wet, sucking kisses along his flesh. "S-So, um, wh-why now, anyway?" A thought caused him to tense, and he tightened his grip on the swing's ropes. "You h-heard I'm looking into starting a business here, didn't you?"

Brian paused in his ministrations.

Monty turned a little, allowing him to meet Brian's dark-eyed gaze.

"Yes," Brian replied, obviously being honest. His warm regard sent a wash of heat through Monty's torso, even as his words caused a niggle of disappointment in his gut. Brian continued to hold his gaze as he stated, "But I'd realized what a coward I was being and that I wanted to see if you'd give me another chance before finding out about that."

"You did?"

Monty couldn't help how breathless he sounded. Brian

might have stopped kissing his neck, but he hadn't stopped rubbing his hands over Monty's front, and it was creating a riot of tingles through his body. His nipples had tightened, aching pleasantly, and his prick had quickly thickened within his shorts.

"Yes," Brian confirmed, his voice deep and firm. "I did. I'd planned to come here regardless after my shift, but Ryan and Carl tracked me down in the breakroom."

Even knowing he should ask about Brian's claim about his father, Monty still couldn't focus on it. "You're making it really hard to think," he admitted softly. Seeing Brian's smirk as well as the heat in his dark eyes, Monty murmured, "And you're really pleased by that."

"I am," Brian admitted as his expression turned hungry. "Want me to help you relax before we talk serious shit?"

As Brian spoke, he lowered one hand and teased along the side of Monty's straining shaft. That gentle glide, even through his shorts, drew a gasp from him. Brian's eyelids slid to half-mast as he growled softly and did it again.

"God, I do love how responsive you are, Monty," Brian rumbled huskily. "Tell me yes, *Hotwheels*."

"N-Not *Hotwheels* anymore," Monty mumbled, glancing toward his crutches.

"Hmmm, you're right." Brian's expression managed to appear contemplative even through his hunger. "Guess I'll have to think of something else." Before Monty could come up with any offers, Brian pressed his thumb into the sensitive flesh beneath Monty's crown. "I want to touch your cock, Monty," Brian stated bluntly. "I want to tug you and suck you and give you pleasure."

Monty figured he should say no. Letting Brian tug him off that first day together had been slutty enough. But he'd been lusting after this man for weeks, and he just couldn't resist his offer.

124

With his erection twitching with need and his balls heavy and aching, Monty whispered, "Pleeease. God, yes, please."

"You never need to beg, baby," Brian purred, easing around him on the swing so he faced Monty. "There are so many things I want to do to you."

Sliding one hand into Monty's hair, Brian brought their lips together. He didn't wait for him to open to him. Instead, Brian pushed his tongue between his lips, taking what he wanted.

Monty was more than on board with the tongue-play and opened wider. Meeting the other man's appendage, he teased his own along it. He relished the man's masculine flavor as Brian dominated his mouth, ravishing him, as if he was a drowning man and Monty's kiss was a life preserver.

Feeding Brian a moan, Monty released the ropes and reached for him. He gripped his soon-to-be lover's shirt and clutched him with both hands. Holding tightly, Monty trusted Brian to keep him steady on the swing as he continued to revel in the man's kiss.

By the time Brian broke the kiss, Monty's lungs were screaming for air. He panted harshly as shudders of need racked him. His cock leaked in his shorts, and he feared he would blow before Brian could even do anything.

"God, your kiss . . ." Monty began.

"Name's Brian," he teased with a feral smile. "Never been mistaken for god before."

Monty snorted as he narrowed his eyes. "Ass."

"I do have a nice one, thank you," Brian replied with an eyebrow waggle. "But I won't let you have it until your cast is off."

Gasping, Monty whispered, "You're a switch?"

"Mmm-hmmm," Brian rumbled. Lowering his hand to Monty's groin, he cupped his erection through the fabric of his shorts. "Sure hope you are, too."

"Yessss." Groaning, Monty tried to buck into Brian's hold,

but the move caused him to begin to slip from the swing. Tightening where he clutched Brian's shirt, Monty nearly yanked it sideways as he muttered, "Shit."

"Easy, baby," Brian murmured, moving both hands to Monty's hips to steady him. "No falling now."

Monty grimaced as he looked away. "Yeah," he muttered. "That wouldn't be sexy."

"You sprawled on the ground would be more than sexy," Brian countered, nuzzling his nose along Monty's jaw until he could nip his ear. "I'm sure it'd be the most erotic, drool-worthy view I've ever seen. And I look forward to seeing it, but not today." Brian suckled Monty's earlobe, drawing a gasp from him as Monty trembled. Releasing his flesh, Brian purred, "I won't do anything to set back your healing, baby, so move your hands back to the swing's ropes."

With his brain clouded with lust, it took Monty a few heartbeats to process Brian's words. Then it took another couple of seconds to gather enough coordination to do it. Slowly, Monty peeled his fingers from Brian's shirt and regripped the ropes.

"There we go." Brian pecked a number of kisses along Monty's jaw as he eased his head back a little. Meeting Monty's gaze with lust in his eyes, Brian grinned. "Hold on tight, baby."

Monty couldn't find his tongue as he watched Brian look down. Following the other man's gaze, he gasped as Brian slid his bronzed hand beneath the elastic waist of his shorts. Feeling Brian grip his length in his big, hot hand, Monty groaned as his erection throbbed in his grip.

Brian used his other hand to pull the waistband of his shorts forward, then down. Rotating his wrist, he cradled Monty's balls, revealing his groin to his feral gaze. Brian gently rolled his sensitive sack as he began jacking him.

The cooling evening air teased Monty's hot flesh in counterpoint to Brian's warm, firm grip. His balls immediately felt hot and tight, and a bead of pre-cum oozed from his flushed head. When Brian used his thumb to massage his frenulum, more fluid pooled up to join the first bead.

"Brian," Monty whined, squeezing the ropes even more as his gut tightened. "Please."

"I didn't get to see you last time," Brian whispered, meeting his gaze with lust-filled eyes. "You're beautiful."

Brian didn't seem to need a response, and Monty appreciated that, because he wouldn't have been able to get words past his throat. In the next instant, Brian bent over his lap. Moving his hand to grip Monty's base, Brian swallowed his prick damn near to the root.

Shouting his pleasure, Monty dug the heel of his right foot into the dirt. He barely managed to remember not to do the same to his casted leg. Still, using his arms, Monty managed to crunch up, nearly raising his ass from the swing.

Immediately, Brian popped off his prick, and Monty groaned with disappointment.

"Relax your ass back down, Monty," Brian ordered gruffly, peering up at him. "I won't have you falling."

Monty moaned but carefully did as he'd been ordered.

"Good." Brian continued to fondle Monty's balls as he rubbed his other hand up under his shirt to rub along his abdominals. "I need you safe, baby, so try to stay in your seat." Brian's expression held a mixture of need, desire, and concern. "Okay?"

Panting softly, Monty managed to nod as he whispered, "Okay."

"I know you're wound up," Brian rumbled as he began lowering his head. "I want to drink you. Come for me."

Upon hearing those words, Monty sucked in a surprised gasp. A second later, he let it out in a cry of delight as Brian wrapped his lips around his crown once more. The heat and suction on his cock's head shot zings of pleasure down his shaft to his balls. With the way Brian continued to massage his testicles, they quickly began to tighten.

Monty had no idea how Brian had figured out his sack was a hot spot, but he couldn't hold back his moan of delight. Tipping his head back, he gritted his teeth, trying to hold back his orgasm. The sensation of Brian bobbing on his erection just felt so amazing, and he didn't want the experience to end just yet.

Except, then Brian lifted his hand higher on his chest. He gripped a nipple and pinched lightly. The zing went straight to his groin.

Goose bumps broke out on the sensitive flesh there, and Brian scraped his thumbnail around the base of Monty's shaft while still gripping his sack.

Unable to stop it, Monty did exactly as Brian encouraged. His release swelled through him, and he moaned his lover's name as he poured spurt after spurt of seed into his waiting, still-sucking mouth. Shudders racked Monty as Brian continued to lightly suckle him, stimulating him, making it feel as if his orgasm went on and on.

Monty's senses soared, and sparks danced across his vision. His breaths came in ragged pants as he tried to get enough air into his body. Whispering Brian's name, Monty felt as if he was floating.

Finally, Brian eased off his softening prick. He peered up at Monty, and his smile looked like the cat that ate the cream. At that thought, Monty couldn't hold in a soft giggle.

Brian's smile widened. "Damn, I like that sound."

Feeling his cheeks heat for a different reason, Monty glanced away. "Uh, okay."

Continuing to grin widely, Brian told him, "Don't feel self-conscious, baby. I love knowing I gave you such pleasure."

"You definitely did that," Monty confirmed. When he saw Brian wince as he adjusted himself, drawing attention to the ridgeline of his jeans-covered erection, he felt his mouth water. "Stand up here, and let me help you with that."

Brian stared at him with narrowed eyes for one heartbeat, two, and Monty worried he would be denied. Then his lover's grin returned, and he rose to his feet.

"I'd be a fool to deny that request," Brian stated huskily.

"Yes, you would," Monty confirmed, reaching for Brian's fly. As he made short work of the button, then gripped the tab of the zipper, Monty peered at Brian through his lashes. "And I'm certain you're no fool, officer."

Chuckling roughly, Brian threaded his fingers through Monty's hair. "I don't know about that," he whispered as he stared down at him. "I was a damn fool to try to resist you, baby." His expression sobered as he whispered, "I'm sorry."

Not wanting to dwell on what couldn't be changed, Monty told him, "We can't change the past. Let's just focus on the future."

Brian's smile warmed Monty's heart. "I can do that." Then his look turned lascivious. "Suck me, beautiful."

With a smirk of his own, Monty rolled his eyes. He did do as Brian requested, however. Monty eased the zipper down, revealing his lover's navy-blue boxers. With a pull and tug, he had both items halfway down Brian's thighs.

Monty hummed at the sight of Brian's thick shaft bouncing free of its confinement. The pale-brown erection before him didn't disappoint. He guessed it to be at least eight inches with just the right amount of girth that it would fill him so good without splitting him wide open.

"Gorgeous," Monty purred as he wrapped his fingers around the base. He took a few seconds to lightly jack him, tracing the swollen vein running the length with his thumb. Hearing Brian's low groan created a sense of power to surge through him, and Monty licked his lips with a bead of pre-cum that oozed from Brian's slit. "Damn."

Continuing to learn the feel of Brian's heavy prick with one hand, Monty turned his attention to his lover's balls. The large sack already appeared high and tight to his body, betraying the man's need. With his free hand, Monty carefully caressed the soft flesh, gauging his new lover's sensitivity.

"Fuck!" Brian barked, his hips jerking. "Please, baby. Please suck me." His voice was low and rough, telling Monty of his need just as surely as his words did. "Sucking you tasted so good. Got me so hot." Even a hint of a whine entered the big man's voice. "Need so bad."

Monty didn't leave his lover hanging. Moving the hand not teasing his ball sack to Brian's hip for balance, he leaned forward and wrapped his lips around his lover's cock. Monty managed to take half of him in the first pass as he enjoyed the weight and feel of the man on his tongue. Brian's flesh was hot and firm within his mouth, and his pre-cum had just the perfect hint of tang to it.

Wanting more of that, looking forward to tasting Brian's full flavor, Monty sucked hard as he bobbed back to the head. He immediately reversed directly and sank all the way down. Burying his nose in Brian's lightly-haired groin, Monty lodged his lover's crown in his throat and swallowed.

Brian roared his pleasure and cradled Monty's head in one hand.

Looking up, Monty saw he gripped the swing's rope with his other in a nearly white-knuckled grip. The fingers holding his head flexed and relaxed lightly, as if he were barely controlling himself. Brian's feral grimace also betrayed his lover's need.

Monty knew Brian was worried about him—being injured and all—and as he went to work bobbing and sucking, doing his best to blow his lover's mind, he silently vowed that, one day, he would make Brian lose that control.

A few seconds later, Brian barked Monty's name as his balls pulled away from Monty's teasing fingertips, drawing even tighter to his groin. His lover's cock twitched in his mouth, twice, before the first burst of seed coated the back of Monty's throat, almost making him choke.

Quickly swallowing as he backed off, Monty prepared for the next burst. The power of Brian's ejaculations told him exactly how pent-up his new lover had been, and pride swelled through him. Monty didn't know how long Brian's dry spell had been, but he loved that he was ending it with him.

Rolling Brian's seed over his tongue, Monty hummed even as he continued to suckle, urging the other man to give him more.

Absolutely delicious.

CHAPTER SIXTEEN

"So . . . my trapeze line was cut?"

Brian hated the pain he heard in Monty's voice. Still, he wasn't going to lie to the man. "Mostly, yes," he confirmed. "Your father paid Byron to make you have an *accident*." Brian made air quotes before returning his arms back around the slender male.

After their mutual blowjobs, they'd returned to the house and ordered Chinese. While waiting for it to arrive, they'd curled up on the sofa. The TV was on a classical music channel, and Brian was finally explaining everything he'd learned from the detectives.

"Damn. Byron? That's crazy." Monty shook his head in clear disbelief. "He'd always seemed like such a nice guy." With a frown, Monty muttered, "I mean, I knew he had aspirations to take over my position, but he's really not as good as me."

"Well, he must have thought, with you out of the way, he had a chance," Brian told him. "Right now, he's in a jail in Amarillo waiting transfer back to Birmingham, since that's where the crime happened." After a second of hesitation, Brian added, "The detective on the case is going to contact you about pressing charges and testifying at his trial, but Ryan asked him to give him a day so we could tell you instead."

Nodding, Monty told him, "Yeah. Yeah, of course I'll press charges." He scoffed as he muttered, "I sure wouldn't want him getting away with that shit." A tremble worked through

Monty as he whispered, "I could have died. If he did it again, whoever may not be so lucky, and I'd have to live with that on my conscience."

Brian squeezed Monty tighter as he pressed a kiss to his lover's temple. "I'm glad we'll get him off the street." Then he revealed, "He'll be put away for a while for attempted murder . . . along with your father."

"My father?" Monty snapped his attention to Brian. "What do you mean?"

Sighing, Brian explained to his lover, "Because your father paid Byron to do it, he's going to be charged, too."

"Shit," Monty hissed, staring at him with wide eyes. "Right. Of course. It's just . . . that's crazy. That's—" Then he deflated as he sighed. "God, I guess I can believe it. It was probably how he knew I was in the hospital. Byron would have told him I hadn't died. Makes sense."

"I'm sorry, baby," Brian murmured, his heart hurting for his lover. *God, this man is my lover. Finally.* Brian really liked thinking of Monty that way. "There's an APB out on your father. Carl or Ryan are supposed to message me once he's in custody."

"Okay." Monty sighed deeply as he snuggled against him. His voice came out soft when he asked, "Can you stay with me until he's caught?"

"Just try to pry me away," Brian declared.

Brian had no intention of going anywhere until the man that wanted Monty dead was off the streets.

"Why?" Monty asked, his voice sounding vacant. "I mean, sure, he's wanted this place for years, but why now?"

"Your father's in debt up to his eyeballs," Brian explained, rubbing Monty's opposite arm absently. "He's made some seriously bad investment deals, and he was about to lose his house, so he borrowed money from the wrong kind of people." Shaking his head, Brian told him, "The kind of people that you don't miss payments to, and he doesn't have it." He peered into Monty's beautiful hazel eyes as he explained, "I imagine in his mind, getting rid of you and showing that he had the money to pay back his debts would buy him the time to collect his inheritance and get the heat off his back."

"Damn," Monty muttered. "If he'd just told me, I would have helped him."

Lifting a hand to cradle Monty's jaw, Brian grimaced. "No, baby. Even if your father somehow managed to swallow his pride to ask, he's not the kind of person you help." When he saw Monty's brows furrow, he knew a rebuttal was coming. Brian quickly reminded him, "You got a restraining order on Cornelian for a reason. You recognized that he was a danger to you. If you gave him money, he would just keep coming back."

Monty sighed deeply as he nuzzled into Brian's hand. "You're right," he whispered. Meeting Brian's gaze, Monty repeated, "I know you're right." His sadness shown from his hazel eyes. "I just hate to think that my own father would stoop to such behavior."

"I'm sorry I'm the one who had to tell you," Brian stated, for lack of anything better to say. No one wanted to think the man who'd helped bring him into the world was out to get him. Trying to lighten the mood, Brian offered, "You can have my family, but after meeting them on Sunday, you may not want them."

"Meeting them on Sunday?" Monty sounded shocked.

Hearing the doorbell ring, Brian rose from his seat. "That'll be the Chinese. Wanna eat in here or in the dining room?" he asked as he started toward the archway that led toward the hall. "And family dinners are every second Sunday of the month, and that's in just a few days."

"And you want me to go already?"

Brian could still hear the disbelief in Monty's tone, so he

turned back and hurried to his side. "Of course, I do," he de-clared as he pressed a hard kiss to his lips. Hearing the door-bell ring again, Brian started walking backward as he headed out of the room. He held Monty's gaze so his lover could see how serious he was. "My mother will be ecstatic that I'm fi-nally seeing someone, and I know she'll love you."

"Okay," Monty murmured. Although he didn't sound completely convinced. "I've, uh, never met a guy's family be-fore." His cheeks were darkening to a gorgeously fetching pink color. "I hope I don't embarrass you."

Shaking his head, Brian exited the room and headed to-ward the front. "You won't," he called, turning his head as he spoke, so his voice would carry back to his lover. "Just be yourself." With a laugh, Brian added, "I'm the one who has to worry about embarrassing stories."

Brian reached the door and flipped the lock. When he heard Monty yell, "Don't forget the baby pictures," he chuck-led as he opened the door.

The click of a hammer filled the air, and Brian instantly so-bered as he found himself staring down the barrel of a re-volver. He felt as if his heart skipped a beat, and he took a reflexive step backward. Of course, the man he recognized as Cornelian took a step forward, moving into the house.

"Montgomery!" Cornelian yelled, his cold hazel eyes glar-ing at Brian. "Get out here, or I'm going to shoot your faggot friend in the head." As Cornelian spoke, he stretched his arm toward Brian. In a low voice, he hissed, "Keep backing up."

Brian obeyed, doing as the gunman ordered. Even as his pulse sped up and he lifted his hands, palms out, in the uni-versal *don't shoot* sign, he took in everything about the man before him. He saw the angry curl of Cornelian's lips and the slight flush to his face. Cornelian held the gun in a steady hand, telling Brian the man was comfortable with the weapon.

Cornelian also had his finger resting against the trigger guard but not on the trigger itself.

Brian knew it wouldn't take much to change that.

"F-Father?" Monty called, a tremor in his voice.

"That's right, you fucker," Cornelian called, sneering. "You couldn't just die like you should have, and now you've fucked up my life." His right eye twitched, and his cheeks began to darken as his rage rose. "You're not gonna get away with it, though, you little shit."

Oh, hell no.

Brian could hear Monty's crutches tapping on the floor of the den, telling him his lover was approaching. Not wanting his sweet acrobat in the line of fire, he searched for an opening. A second later, Brian spotted it.

Cornelian reached beside him and grabbed the front door, using plenty of force to slam it shut. That caused the arm holding the gun on Brian to swing left for just an instant.

Capitalizing on that, Brian stepped forward as he brought his arms together. He grabbed the barrel of the revolver in one hand. With his other, Brian slapped at Cornelian's wrist.

The momentum caused Cornelian to lose his grip on the weapon even as he managed to pull the trigger. The shot went wide, missing Brian, who continued to grip the weapon by the barrel. At the same time, he gripped the wrist he'd slapped and yanked, and Cornelian stumbled toward him.

With ease born of practice, Brian spun Cornelian, tugging his arm behind his back. He shoved the man into the wall. Dropping the gun, Brian quickly snagged Cornelian's free arm and forced it behind his back as well.

Even as Cornelian struggled, Brian easily countered him. He kept his focus on Monty's father while listening to his lover approach.

"Brian?" Monty murmured. "Are you okay? Are you shot?"

Shaking his head, Brian assured, "I'm fine. He missed."

Taking a chance, he glanced Monty's way. "What about you?"

"I'm fine," Monty told him. "I heard that shot and was so scared." He glanced toward the gun on the floor while nibbling his lip. "Um, what should I do?"

The silent question was clear enough. Should Monty grab the gun?

"Don't touch it, baby," Brian ordered softly. "Will you unbuckle my belt, please?"

Monty gave him a playful smile even as he crutched closer. "Now is hardly the time."

As Brian chuckled, Cornelian snarled and tried to buck out of Brian's hold, but he easily subdued him.

With a grin and a wink, Brian promised, "Later, baby. My cuffs are in my SUV."

Nodding, Monty told him, "I kinda figured that's what you actually meant."

"Love your teasing," Brian told him.

Feeling Monty's fingers working his belt, Brian mentally willed his body not to respond. It really wasn't the time, but it was tough. After all, Brian loved having Monty's hands on his body . . . for any reason.

When Monty finished tugging it free, Brian switched to holding Cornelian with one hand so he could take the belt. Once more, Cornelian tried to wrestle free. Brian used his body weight, pressing his chest to Cornelian's back as he quickly wrapped his belt around the asshole's wrists.

"Stay still," Brian warned gruffly, yanking the belt tight. "Or your circulation will suffer."

"Fucking faggot," Cornelian snarled. "I'll get free."

"You really won't," Brian countered before looking Monty's way again. "Can you call Ryan, please, baby?"

Monty nodded. "My phone's in the other room."

Swiveling his hips, Brian dipped his chin to indicate his phone in his pocket. "Use mine."

After tugging it free, Monty obeyed.

Thirty minutes later, Brian stood on the front porch with his arm wrapped around Monty's shoulders. He clutched his lover close as the adrenaline slowly eased from his body. Brian watched Carl place Cornelian in the back of a police cruiser.

"You all okay?" Ryan asked, coming up behind them. The other detective had been collecting Cornelian's gun as well as digging the bullet out of the wall.

Brian nodded. "I'm good." He squeezed Monty's opposite upper arm. "What about you, baby?"

"I'm good," Monty replied softly.

Ryan stopped beside them. "Nice moves, Brian. You learn that slap-away technique in the academy?"

Smirking, Brian admitted, "Uh, no. A movie, actually."

Barking a laugh, Ryan shook his head. "Well, whatever works."

"Is my mom involved?" Monty asked suddenly.

Ryan sighed deeply. "Afraid so." Then he grimaced and added, "We don't know *how involved*, but she at least knew about Cornelian's plans. We already have her in custody," Ryan assured. "So you won't be getting a visit from her."

Brian felt Monty's shoulders droop, and he hated the crappy hand that his lover had been dealt in regards to family. Wrapping his second arm around Monty, he turned his lover and tucked him against his chest. He pressed a chaste kiss to his man's temple.

"Like I told you before," Brian whispered into his ear. "You can have my family. They'll love you almost as much as I do."

Monty's head snapped up so fast, he nearly cracked his forehead into Brian's nose.

"You love me?" Monty whispered, staring up at him with wide eyes.

"Uhhhh—" Brian snapped his mouth shut.

Wait. Yeah. I did say that.

Ryan chuckled, patting him on the shoulder. "I'll keep you guys posted," he assured before heading down the walk toward where Carl was waiting.

"Thanks, Ryan," Brian responded vacantly, continuing to stare into Monty's gorgeous hazel eyes. He'd always loved looking at them, and he had a funny feeling that he always would. Lifting a hand to Monty's jaw, Brian teased his thumb over his lover's smooth cheek. "Yes, Monty," he stated, knowing Monty deserved the truth. "I have a bad habit of falling fast and hard for someone, and that's why the idea of you leaving the area hurt so much. I wanted you here." Before Monty could respond, Brian quickly told him, "That's why I realized that I needed to give you a reason to stay. Maybe I wouldn't be enough, but I had to damn well try."

"You're more than enough," Monty replied, a shy smile curving his lips. "I-I love you, too." A happy-sounding giggle bubbled from Monty's lips. "Never been in love before. I-I like it."

Chuckling, Brian nodded. "Me, too." Dipping his head, he pecked a kiss to Monty's delectable lips. When he lifted his head, he grinned at his lover. "Come on. Let's head back inside. We have Chinese to eat." Waggling his brows, Brian added, "Do you have a problem with eating in bed?"

"Not at all," Monty told him. After sweeping his gaze over Brian's frame, he gave Brian a lecherous look. "As long as you're naked."

Groaning, Brian guided his lover back into the house. "I like the way you think," he declared, closing and locking the door behind him.

Brian grabbed the bag of Chinese, which had been delivered while they'd been waiting for the police.

After a peck on Monty's temple, Brian told him, "I'm going to grab drinks, plates, napkins, and silverware." He gave his lover's ass an appreciative pat followed by a squeeze. "Be right there."

Monty began crutching away from him, somehow managing to shake his ass in the process. "Hurry."

"Knew you'd be a minx," Brian growled, smacking Monty's ass again.

"Only for you," Monty replied breathily.

"Perfect."

Then Brian rushed past his lover to gather what they needed. He could hardly wait to enjoy . . . everything Monty had to offer, for as long as possible.

And I'm gonna make sure that's a long damn time.

With that vow in mind, Brian hurried to catch up with his lover.

ABOUT THE AUTHOR

Charlie started writing fantasy when she was eight, and after stumbling onto her first erotic romance at age nineteen, she realized her true calling. She now focuses on writing gay erotic romance, normally of the paranormal variety, with heroes of all kinds. With the help and support of her husband, Charlie finally fulfilled one of her life-long goals . . . move to acreage with her horses. You can often find her curled up with her laptop and a cup of tea or glass of wine, creating her next adventure. Charlie enjoys exploring the mountains of her new Oregon home on horseback, 4-wheeler, or motorcycle.

She can be reached at ch.richards2010@yahoo.com

Or visit her at www.charlie-richards.com.